HARD EDGE

PAMELA CLARE

WWW.PAMELACLARE.COM

HARD EDGE

PAMELA

USA TODAY BESTSELLING AUTHOR

CLARE

Hard Edge
A Cobra Elite novel

Published by Pamela Clare, 2020

Cover Design by © Jaycee DeLorenzo/Sweet 'N Spicy Designs
Cover photo: _italo_

Copyright © 2020 by Pamela Clare

ISBN: 978-1-7335251-9-0

This book is dedicated to the memory of Abuelita Isabel and to the people of Venezuela, wherever they find themselves in the world today.

ACKNLOWLEDGEMENTS

Thanks as always to Michelle White, Benjamin Alexander, Jackie Turner, Shell Ryan, and Pat Egan Fordyce for their support during the writing of this book. Special thanks to Shell Ryan for a last-minute proofread.

Additional thanks to Benjamin for sharing his firearms expertise.

Heartfelt thanks to Andrea Ferrer for sharing her life in Venezuela with me and for helping me to get the details of the culture and language right. Thanks, too, to Arlene and Beatrice Ríos Ramírez for making sure I have my Boricua profanity down. I don't want to say "coño" when it should clearly be "puñeta."

1
———

September 6
El Vigía, Venezuela

"Gracias, Hermana. Dios te bendiga." *Thank you, Sister. God bless you.*

Sister María Catalina stood in the shelter of a timber awning outside the Mission of Our Lady of Coromoto, helping distribute food to the hungry. She handed a woman, a mother of four, a box that held a pound of rice, a pound of dried beans, some potatoes, powdered milk, and bananas. It would last only a few days, but it was something.

"God bless you and your family," she said.

The young woman was so thin and undernourished that María thought she might need help carrying the box. She and her children had arrived at the mission this morning, their eyes dull from hunger. They hadn't eaten in four days.

Somehow, the young mother shouldered the box, her thin arms wiry and strong.

"You must eat, too." María handed a banana to each of

the woman's children. "Who will take care of your little ones if you become too weak or sick?"

"*Sí, Hermana*, but I cannot listen to my children cry. We are on our way to Colombia, where my husband has work. Life will be better there."

It had been the same every day since María had arrived at the Mission outside El Vigía six months ago, a stream of desperate humanity in need of food, medicine, and, most of all, hope. More than a million people had fled to Colombia, while millions more had gone elsewhere—to the US, Europe, or other nations in the Americas.

It broke María's heart to witness the suffering of Venezuela's people. So many going hungry. Families left destitute and divided as people sought refuge in whichever nation would take them. Cancer patients like her Grandmother Isabel dying without treatment or pain relief.

When her parents had been in college in the 1980s, Venezuela had been a wealthy country with a robust middle class. After the *Caracazo* in 1989, when government troops had killed hundreds of protestors on the streets, they had emigrated to the United States with their three older children. María had been born Gabriela Aliana Marquez a year later in Miami. She'd grown up in Florida, speaking both English and Spanish and getting her love of Venezuelan food and culture through her mother's milk. She had visited her grandparents every year—until her parents decided it was too dangerous to return.

Now, Venezuela was an economic ruin.

But that's why María had come. She wanted to do her part to change things, to help make life better in the land her parents had once called home.

She picked up the smallest child, a little girl who needed

a bath. "You should stay for a few days, rest and eat, and then move on when you feel stronger."

The woman stared at her, fragile hope in her eyes. "Is that possible?"

María smiled and tried to convey a serenity she did not feel. "With God, all things are possible."

She called to Oscar, a boy of twelve who'd come to stay with them when his parents had been killed in the crossfire of a fight between protestors and el SEBIN—Venezuela's intelligence service that behaved more like death squads or *ladrones con placa*—criminals with badges. "Oscar, can you run and speak with Sister María José and ask her to find a place for this woman and her four children?"

"*¡Sí, Hermana!*" Oscar jumped to his feet and dashed off.

María settled the woman and her children indoors and went back to distributing food, the line dwindling at last. As the newest member of the mission, it was her job to do whatever was asked of her. Mostly, that meant cleaning, working in the kitchen, and helping to feed the people who came to them for help. Her day started before dawn with prayers and ended only when the work was done, long after dark.

From behind her came the sound of American English.

The journalist.

Dianne Connolly was visiting today with a photographer and two bodyguards. Mother Narcisa escorted them around the mission, answering her questions in heavily accented English.

Mother Narcisa stepped outside, the reporter, photographer, and their bodyguards following. "This is where we distribute food to those in need."

María made eye contact with Mother Narcisa, who gave

her a slight nod, granting her permission to go. María couldn't risk being interviewed or photographed.

Mother Narcisa's words followed her as she walked inside. "That was Sister María Catalina. She came to us from a cloister of Poor Clares in Peru. In keeping with her vows, she prefers as hidden a life as possible."

"We can't interview her?" the reporter asked.

"No, but there are other sisters here who—"

The roar of a car engine. Shouts. Gunshots.

Screams.

María ran back to the door—and stared.

The bodyguards lay dead on the ground. Four men with automatic weapons and bandanas on their faces climbed out of a white van and headed for the journalists.

An abduction.

Mother Narcisa knelt beside the two slain bodyguards, blood on her trembling hands, shock on her face.

Pulse tripping, María stepped over one man's body, put herself between the attackers and the journalist, and did her best to look as imposing as the Sisters from her Catholic school days. "Señores, this is a mission! It is sacred ground. Put away your weapons and—"

"What have we here?" One of the attackers stepped up to her, all but his eyes hidden behind a bandana. He reached out, took hold of her black veil, rubbed the cloth between his fingers. "You're too pretty to be a nun—and helpless to stop me."

The men behind him laughed.

María wasn't afraid of him. She took a step back, glanced over her shoulder at the reporter, who stood wide-eyed, her back pressed against the wall, her photographer shielding her, the terror on their faces putting rage in María's heart.

She met the assailant's gaze. "Think about what you're

doing. You've already murdered two men. Kidnapping the reporter would be another mortal sin—and will bring the United States down on you. Is that what—"

With no warning, the man bent down and threw her over his shoulder. "The rest of you—get the gringos."

He climbed into the van and dropped María onto the floor of the vehicle, driving the breath from her lungs.

It took a moment for reality to hit home.

They were abducting her, too.

¡Madre de Dios!

Mother of God.

September 8

DYLAN CRUZ SAT on Cobra International Security's private jet with the rest of the crew somewhere over the Atlantic Ocean. They'd spent the past two weeks running security for US State Department officials on a mission to Ouagadougou, the capital city of Burkina Faso. The assignment had gone off without a hitch, but it was good to be on their way home again—even if that meant listening to more of Thor Isaksen's stories.

If even half the shit he said about his years with Denmark's Sirius Sled Patrol was true, the man was a certified badass—or just plain loco.

"The storm came up fast, caught us in the open," said Isaksen. "The temperatures dropped to minus seventy, and the wind was so strong we couldn't put up our tent. The dogs were restless and growling. We staked the team, dug a snow cave, and crawled inside—no food, no stove."

"Minus seventy?" Cruz had faced more than his share of

freezing nights in the mountains of Afghanistan during his decade with the SEALs, but he'd never been in that kind of cold. "That would freeze exposed skin in minutes."

Isaksen went on. "After we settled in, we noticed a sound, like someone snoring. But we were in the middle of northeastern Greenland. There was no one else around."

"It wasn't one of you—another sled team?" asked Malik Jones, a former Army Ranger and Dylan's best bud. "Man, that's creepy."

"It took us a minute to realize that we'd dug into a snowbank where a mother polar bear had made her den. She was a few feet away, separated from us by snow. The dogs had smelled her, but we were so distracted by the storm that we didn't pick up their warning."

"She was hibernating," said Lev Segal, a former operative with Israeli counterterrorism forces.

Isaksen shook his head. "Polar bears don't hibernate. She was just asleep. All she had to do was dig a little with those big paws, and she could have eaten both of us for dinner."

"What did you do?" Elizabeth Shields stared at Isaksen. If she believed him, there was a good chance he was telling the truth. She'd come to Cobra from the CIA and was a counterterrorism analyst.

"We got the hell out of there and set up camp a few kilometers away."

"A bottle of whiskey says he's full of shite," said Quinn McManus, a grin on his bearded face. The big Scot, who had served with Britain's Special Air Service, had married Elizabeth this past July, and the two were sickeningly happy.

Isaksen grinned. "Why would I lie?"

"Maybe you were hallucinating." Derek Tower, one of the co-owners of Cobra, hadn't joined in the conversation until now, his face buried in his tablet. "Out there in the cold for three months at a time, just two guys and a pack of sled dogs—it must play tricks on a man's mind."

Tower had served as a Green Beret and knew all about mind tricks.

Isaksen's expression grew serious. "We wondered the same thing."

The conversation drifted after that, and Dylan tuned out, tried to sleep. This routine had been his life since he'd made the Teams—getting spun up at a moment's notice and then flying home or moving on to the next job. He'd learned to sleep whenever and wherever he could.

When he woke, it was dark outside his window. Across from him, Shields slept with her head on McManus' shoulder, the two of them sharing a single blanket.

Are you jealous, pendejo?

Nah, he was done with serious relationships. He loved women, but Valeria had proven to him that men in his line of work were better off single. Thank God he'd only been engaged to her and hadn't married her. Even so, what she and Kruger had done had torn his world apart, ending his SEAL career and forcing him to start again.

His mother wanted him to move home to Puerto Rico, get a job at the pharmaceutical plant in Arecibo, and marry a nice Boricua girl. As much as Dylan loved Puerto Rico, he was afraid that the boredom of an ordinary life would kill him. Besides, he wasn't interested in marriage.

Was he lonely sometimes?

He pushed the thought away. He had women in his life —if the women he met through Tinder counted. They got what they wanted, and so did he.

A hand came down on his shoulder.

Tower stood beside him. "Cruz, you, Jones, and Segal need to come with me."

Dylan glanced at the others to see if they knew what this was about, but they were clearly as much in the dark as he. He stood and followed Tower and the others to the small conference room at the rear of the plane.

Tower shut the door. "I just heard from Corbray."

Javier Corbray, Tower's partner, typically worked in Washington, D.C., representing Cobra's interests with Congress and Pentagon officials.

"We've been tasked with a top-secret recon and rescue mission, and you three are going to be our recon team. We'll land in Denver in a few hours. Get some sleep and be ready to leave again by oh-eight-hundred hours. We'll fill you in tomorrow morning."

"Can you say where we're headed?" Segal asked.

"Venezuela."

Dylan gave a low whistle. "Are you serious?"

Tower was always serious. "We have to keep this completely off the radar."

He didn't need to explain. Venezuela's current regime had an adversarial relationship with the US, accusing Washington of meddling in the country's affairs. The US, meanwhile, accused the Venezuelan government of drug trafficking. If US forces were found on the ground there, it would create a political firestorm. That's undoubtedly why they were sending in Cobra operatives rather than Delta Force or one of the Teams.

Jones didn't seem troubled by this. "No polar bears there."

"No polar bears," Tower agreed, "just narco-terrorists, mafiosos, revolutionaries, and trigger-happy secret police."

"I can handle those, boss. But a mama bear? Shit." Jones shook his head.

Segal snorted. "Are you afraid of snakes and spiders, too, brother?"

"Hell, yes, I am."

But Dylan was already thinking about the new job. A secret op in Venezuela. This was going to be interesting.

September 9

MARÍA AWOKE WITH A START, sat up, glanced around her basement prison. The faint light of dawn glowed beyond narrow, barred windows high above the concrete floor. Dianne and her photographer, Tim, were still asleep. An armed guard—one of the men who had abducted them—dozed on a wooden chair propped against the door that was their only exit. In the opposite corner, rats nosed about, looking for a meal.

Revulsion shivered through María. Being abducted was one thing. Being forced to share space with rats—that was something else.

She knelt on the tattered wool blanket that served as her bed, straightened her scapular and veil, pulled her rosary from the knotted rope that bound her waist. Then she crossed herself and began to pray the Divine Mercy chaplet in silence, willing herself to focus on the words of the prayer and not the squeaks coming from the corner. The words came without effort, the recitation clearing her mind, helping her to focus.

Por Su dolorosa Pasión, ten misericordia de nosotros y del mundo entero.

For the sake of His sorrowful Passion, have mercy on us and on the whole world.

She heard when the guard woke, when he got to his feet, when he came to stand in front of her, but she didn't open her eyes. She felt the barrel of his rifle caress her cheek, cold steel against her skin, and still she prayed, not giving him the satisfaction of a reaction. Bullies like him thrived on other people's fear. Besides, if these men had intended to kill her or the other hostages, they'd be dead already.

By the time María had finished her morning prayers, the guard was talking to his girlfriend on his cell phone, and Dianne and Tim were awake. They had to be as hungry as she was. Because they didn't speak Spanish, they were also more afraid and disoriented. María turned her attention to them.

No, this wasn't where she was supposed to be. Being kidnapped and held hostage wasn't what she'd envisioned when she'd taken this assignment. But as long as her abductors respected her status as a religious sister, she could still do her job.

She stood, walked over to kneel before Dianne and Tim. "Did you sleep?"

She spoke with a heavy Spanish accent, certain her safety and her ability to do her job depended on no one knowing that she, too, was a US citizen. Otherwise, her captors would surely try to ransom her, as well.

"A little." Dianne brushed her fingers through her tangled blonde hair. "It's cold at night, and this floor is so hard."

That was the truth.

Tim watched the guard. "Have the bastards said what they want with us yet?"

María lowered her voice to a whisper. "They are holding

you for ransom. I heard them talking about it. Do not be afraid. When they get the money, they will let you go."

She'd also overheard conversations about shipments of potatoes and bananas coming in from Colombia and a few mentions of *el Jefe*—the Boss. She wasn't naïve enough to believe they were really talking about potatoes and bananas.

The actual cargo was cocaine.

For years now, Colombian drug cartels had been operating in Venezuela with the help of officials at the highest levels of government. They used the Mission as cover, transporting drugs hidden beneath much-needed food and medicine. Father Alberto not only knew what they were doing, but also served as their confessor, absolving murderers and drug traffickers of their sins while preaching about the poor and downtrodden.

Sister María loathed him.

As for the identity of *el Jefe*, it was almost certainly Luis Rafael Sánchez Mantilla, the president's brother-in-law. He'd visited the mission more than once, always after a shipment, meeting in private with Father Alberto for spiritual direction—or so Father Alberto claimed. Now it seemed that Sánchez and Sergio de Anda Ruiz, the powerful head of the Andes Cartel, had taken up kidnapping in addition to drug trafficking. Maybe they just wanted the money—or perhaps their goal was to discourage foreign journalists.

"What about you?" Dianne had already apologized to María a half dozen times, as if she were to blame for María's abduction.

María willed herself to smile. "The Church does not pay ransom, but do not worry. I don't believe they will harm me."

Dianne took her hand. "If you hadn't tried to stop them—"

"¡*Cállate!*" the guard shouted. *Shut up!*

María wouldn't let him intimidate her. She stood, turned to face him, scolding him in an unbroken stream of Spanish, invoking his mother, his grandmothers, and the Blessed Virgin before demanding that he bring them all warm water for washing and something to eat and drink. "What would your mamá say if she could see this?"

The scolding had its desired effect, the guard's gaze dropping to the floor before he muttered, "*Sí, Hermana.*"

Then he left them alone.

"I guess you showed him," Tim said.

Dianne stared at her in amazement. "You're not afraid of them."

That wasn't necessarily true, but María refused to admit that.

She smiled. "God is my strength."

2

Dylan poured himself a cup of coffee and made his way to the conference room, Jones and Segal shuffling in behind him, all of them jet lagged as *fuck*.

Tower and Shields were already there, waiting.

Dylan glanced at the empty seats. "Where is everyone else?"

Shields set her coffee mug on the table, her strawberry-blonde hair pulled back in a bun. "This mission is strictly need-to-know."

Jones grinned. "I guess the others don't need to know."

"Not yet." Tower started the meeting. "This tasking comes from the highest levels of the Pentagon. Everything about it is classified. Understood?"

Dylan nodded.

"Good." Tower clicked the remote to turn on the big flat-screen monitor mounted on the wall behind him.

A blurry image of an attractive blond-haired woman filled the screen.

"This is Dianne Connolly, age thirty-nine, a journalist from the LA Times Syndicate. Four days ago, she and photographer Timothy Yang, age 42, were abducted while on assignment." Tower clicked again, and a photo of Yang appeared. "Their two Venezuelan bodyguards were shot and killed."

"Narcos?" Dylan knew a little about the situation in Venezuela.

Tower nodded. "Andes Cartel."

"Shit." Dylan exchanged a glance with Jones. "Those guys don't fuck around."

"Their abductors contacted the US embassy in Brazil. They're demanding ten million dollars US for the pair's release."

"Fuck that." Segal didn't believe in negotiating with terrorists. "If they're giving this job to us, it must mean the Pentagon wants to teach these bastards a lesson."

"Pretty much—but there's more." Tower clicked the remote again, and a photograph of a young nun filled the screen.

Dylan gaped at her, his heart skipping a beat. "*Ah, coño.*" *Damn.*

Malik and Segal stared, too.

She looked like she was in her late twenties with big brown eyes, long lashes, a perfect little nose, and full lips, her brown skin flawless, dark hair showing from beneath her black veil.

"She's what my uncle would call Sister What-a-Waste." Dylan had grown up Catholic, though he hadn't gone to Mass in ages.

Segal snorted. "I never understood the whole celibacy thing."

Tower ignored them. "This is Sister María Catalina. She's a US citizen, age twenty-nine. She was born Gabriela Aliana Marquez in Miami. Her parents are Venezuelan immigrants who left the country due to political unrest. She asked to be transferred to Venezuela from a Franciscan cloister in Peru because she wanted to help the Venezuelan people."

Tower clicked again, showed a blurry photo of what looked like the outside of a church or mission. A white van was parked beside it, men with rifles moving in on their prey. "This is the Mission of Our Lady of Coromoto, where the victims were snatched. The photo was taken with a smartphone from a rooftop across the street. Eye-witnesses, including the nun in charge of the mission, said Sister María tried to stop the abductors and was taken, as well."

Dylan saw her, hands raised as if to stop a man with an automatic rifle.

Jones glared at the screen. "What kind of asshole kidnaps a nun?"

Dylan's fatigue was gone, pushed aside by anger. "The kind that needs a bullet in his brain."

Tower clicked again, and another photo of the mission appeared, Sister María now slung over the shoulder of some *hijoeputa*. "The Church doesn't pay ransom, which may be one reason the Pentagon decided to mount a rescue. Sister María is a US citizen, and they're absolutely determined *not* to leave her in these guys' hands."

Dylan could get behind that.

Tower clicked once more, and a map of Venezuela came up on the screen. "The mission is close to the Colombian border in a village called El Vigía. The sisters distribute food to the poor and offer basic medical care. But the Pentagon has reason to believe that cocaine was being smuggled into the country via those food shipments, thanks to the Andes Cartel ... and this fucker."

An image of an overweight middle-aged man in a suit

and tie filled the screen. Balding, he had meaty features and a fat mustache.

Tower turned the remote over to Shields.

She stood. "Meet Luis Rafael Sánchez Mantilla. He's the brother-in-law of Venezuela's disputed president. The US has long suspected him of colluding with the Andes Cartel to move cocaine through Venezuela to the US market and Europe. He has his own paramilitary forces, which functions as his personal army of hitmen, his private *sicarios*. He calls them the *Guachimanes*—the Watchmen."

Shields then gave them a quick update on the situation in Venezuela—its conflicted presidency, the terrible state of the economy, the lack of food and healthcare, mass emigration, high crime rate, violence. "The government's relationship with the US is strained, to say the least, and any US military presence, even a private company like Cobra, would create an international furor."

Dylan had to ask. "Is there any chance Sister María or the other sisters are part of the drug operation?"

He'd heard of stranger things.

Tower shook his head. "I asked the same question. Our source at the Pentagon says the priest in charge of the Mission is involved, but the nuns reportedly are not."

"How do they know? Where do they get their intel?" Segal asked.

It was a good question.

"They refused to say but assure me it's ironclad." Tower took the remote once more and clicked, bringing up a satellite image. "These intel sources believe that the hostages are together and are being held here—in a warehouse in San Antonio de Los Altos. It's a mountainous area and close to Caracas, the nation's capital."

Shields pointed at the image. "San Antonio sits beside

an area zoned for military use only. You can see here that it has an airfield. The DEA believes that Sánchez and the Andes Cartel might be using this *Zona Militar* to move drugs, but they haven't been able to prove it."

Hostages. A drug cartel. Corrupt government and military officials.

Dylan had been right. This assignment *was* going to be interesting—and dangerous.

The only easy day was yesterday.

He was eager to get airborne, the image of Sister María trying to fend off the assailants fixed in his mind. "So, what's our play?"

SISTER MARÍA SAT on a shipping crate, about to share a meal with the *sicarios* who had kidnapped her. She waited for the men to fill their bowls and find a seat, glaring at those who tried to start eating without saying grace.

The one with the thick glasses they called Topo, or Mole, shifted guiltily under the weight of her gaze but didn't eat.

Who'd known how much authority came with wearing a habit?

They'd let her out of the basement yesterday, allowing her to move freely up and down the stairs and making her their go-between. She took Dianne and Tim their meals, brought clean water for them to drink, and let the guards know when one of them needed to use a restroom. She'd managed to get more blankets, too, making their nights more comfortable. Their abductors had even allowed her to write a letter to her contact, disguised as a letter to the Reverend Mother in Peru, telling him that they were alive and where they were being held.

Her captors had read the letter, of course, but María had been writing in code for the past six months. Of course, she hadn't planned on being kidnapped and didn't have a prearranged code for "we're being held in a warehouse in San Antonio de Los Altos," so she'd had to improvise.

She was grateful for her freedom of movement—and for what it enabled her to see and overhear. She'd memorized the layout of the warehouse and knew the location of every guard post and every exit. She knew, too, that Luis Sánchez was behind the abduction and that he was mad as hell at his men for abducting her with the others. She'd also gleaned that Sánchez would order a military "rescue" once the ransom was paid—an attempt to ingratiate himself with the US government.

Create a crisis and then resolve the crisis while earning millions. For Sánchez, it was win-win-win—except for one tiny problem. María knew the truth.

A sad day for you, Sánchez, you son of a bitch.

"Look at all of you, intimidated by a little nun." The one they called Pitón—the one who'd thrown her over his shoulder—walked in, filled his bowl, and sat, bowing his head and crossing himself with mock piety.

María crossed herself, the men around her, *sicarios* and bandits, doing the same. "Bless us, Lord, and these, Thy gifts, which we are about to receive from Thy bounty. Through Christ, our Lord. Amen."

She crossed herself again, and then began to eat, the men following her example.

"Do you think you're saving our souls, *Hermanita*?" Pitón looked over at her, his gaze tinged with lust.

It was only her being a religious sister that kept him from trying to do more than look—she was certain of that.

"Of course, not." She refused to make eye contact. "Only God can do that."

She ate in silence, her gaze on her food, hoping Pitón would focus his attention elsewhere and that they would all forget she was there.

No such luck.

Pitón spoke with his mouth full. "Don't you worry about what you're missing, *Hermanita*?"

María ignored him.

"When you're alone in your cold bed at night, don't you wonder what it would be like to be the bride of a man instead of the bride of Christ? A pretty girl like you should know a man's love."

She kept her expression serene. "For me, there is no greater joy than fulfilling my calling to serve God and no greater love than the love of God."

"Leave her alone, Pitón, man," muttered Topo.

"Shut up, *mamagüevo*." Pitón glowered at Topo, but he left María alone.

She said a prayer of thanksgiving after the meal then asked one of the men to bring water to heat for washing up. When the bowls and spoons were clean again—or as clean as she could get them—she refilled them and carried them, together with the two bananas she'd managed to hide beneath her habit, downstairs to Dianne and Tim.

"Thank you, Sister." Tim took his bowl and ate hungrily.

Dianne looked disapprovingly at him. "Shouldn't we say grace? I mean, she's a ... I don't want to offend you, Sister."

Tim stopped, mid-chew, his gaze meeting María's.

"I'm not offended. You haven't eaten since breakfast." Aware of the guard standing nearby, a big brute they called

Gordito, María said grace once again, this time in English, carefully removing the bananas from the folds of her tunic and tucking them beneath Dianne's blankets. "Now, please eat."

Dianne had seen the bananas. "Thank you."

The door opened, and Topo appeared, three mugs in hand. He smiled to reveal gold teeth. "Hot coffee."

A cup of coffee cost more than a million bolivars these days, far beyond what most people could pay. But it didn't surprise her that Sánchez's men had access to such luxuries.

María stood, took the mugs from him, and handed one each to Dianne and Tim. "God will bless you for your kindness, Topo."

He shifted, his gaze dropping to the floor. "Do you truly think so?"

"*Sí.*" It would also help if Topo stopped working for a killer, but María didn't say so, instead making the sign of the cross on his forehead. "Father, bless Topo for his compassion and help him to serve only Your will. In the name of the Father, the Son, and the Holy Spirit. Amen."

"*Gracias.*" He exchanged a glance with Gordito, who rolled his eyes, then left them and went back upstairs.

María sat on the floor and sipped her coffee.

Dianne had finished her rice and beans. "I'm sorry you're here with us, Sister, but I don't know what we would do without you."

"Please, don't worry about me." María gave them both what she hoped was a reassuring smile. "I will do all I can to help you."

They were luckier than they knew. The nun who'd been abducted with them wasn't really Sister María Catalina, a devout religious sister. She was Gabriela Márquez, a US citizen and undercover CIA officer.

One way or another, they were going to get out of this alive.

DYLAN MANEUVERED the camera into position, glanced over his shoulder to see Jones pouring himself another mug of coffee. "We might be here for a while, and you're not going to be able to buy more beans, brother."

"Says the guy who's already had two cups." Jones went back to setting up the VPN that would enable them to communicate with Tower and Shields in Bogota.

"If the two of you are going to bicker like an old married couple the entire time we're here, I'm going to need my own place." Segal put the slide back on the Glock 19 he'd been cleaning.

They'd arrived in San Antonio de Los Altos last night, entering through Colombia with fake passports and ID cards, just three men driving a truckload of food and supplies for their families. Their weapons, surveillance, and communication gear lay concealed beneath a fortune in food and basic supplies, including beer and an agave liquor known as *cocuy*. Most of the food was theirs, but the rest of it was for the little black-market operation that would serve as their cover.

Paying with US dollars, they'd gotten an apartment across the street from the warehouse where the hostages were believed to be. Dylan had done the talking, speaking with his best Cuban accent. Jones had brushed up on his Spanish on the flight and could at least swear like a real *venezolano*. Segal was pretending to be from Syria and spoke English and a little Spanish with a convincing Arabic accent.

Dylan focused the camera with its telephoto lens on the warehouse. Part of their job was to record comings and goings and to confirm, if possible, that the hostages were in this location. They wouldn't be able to keep the side entrance under surveillance from this window, but they could at least cover the loading dock and the main doors that faced the street.

Their other job was to gather intel for a rescue. They needed to learn the strength of the enemy and the lay of the land—number of men, kinds of weapons, possible points of ingress—and, if possible, the location of the hostages inside the warehouse. In addition to a telephoto lens, they had a state-of-the-art thermal imaging system that would enable them to peek through windows, though not the warehouse's concrete walls. Every image they took would be sent via VPN to Shields in Colombia for analysis. If they could confirm that the hostages were here, they would work with Tower to start planning a rescue operation, and the rest of the team would be flown in from Denver.

Camera in place, Dylan dragged over a chair and settled in for his shift. "Join the Navy, they said. See the world, they said. Sit on your ass and stare through a camera all damned day—no one said that."

Jones and Segal chuckled.

Recon was important work. It saved lives. But it could be boring as fuck.

He looked through the viewfinder, saw two guys with handguns tucked in the back of their jeans standing guard at the side door. Two more guys stood on the loading dock while a third sat on an overturned bucket, smoking a cigarette.

Dylan snapped their photos. "It would be really great if

one of those bastards in the abduction photos would step outside or if the hostages could just look out a window."

Jones laughed. "Dream on, brother."

Hours passed until Dylan needed to take a bathroom break. "Hey, can one of you take over? I need to hit the head."

Jones left the VPN, which was up and running, and took Dylan's seat. "It's going to rain. Look at those clouds coming over the mountains."

"*En español.* You should keep practicing."

Jones repeated those last words, struggling with the vocabulary. "*Mira las nubes que vienen sobre los montañas.*"

"Las *montañas.* Jesus, man." Dylan walked to the bathroom, shaking his head. "Mountains are feminine."

"Why are they feminine?" Jones called after him.

"How should I know? Maybe they looked like big tits to some Spaniard."

It was raining when Dylan got back to the window.

Jones didn't budge, camera clicking. "Holy shit, man. That's her—the nun."

"What?" Dylan took over, adjusted the focus, and stared. "*¡Puñeta!* You're right."

There she was, unmistakable in her gray tunic and black veil.

"This kind of shit never happens." He clicked shot after shot, hoping to get a clear image of her face. "Turn your head, Sister. Just a little to the left."

As if she could hear him, she turned, looked to her left and then to her right, her hands held out as if to feel the rain, a smile on her pretty face.

Click.

"Yeah, that's her for sure."

Segal leaned in, looked through the viewfinder himself. "It's our lucky day, boys—and hers."

Dylan was still taking photos when a man stepped outside, grabbed the sister by her arm, and dragged her roughly back inside. Dylan snapped a few shots of his face, too, before the bastard disappeared.

There's a bullet in your future, asshole.

Dylan popped out the camera's memory card and handed it to Jones. "Let's get this to Shields right away."

He looked down at the warehouse once more.

Hang on, Sister. We're coming.

3

Pitón shoved Gabriela so hard that she fell to the floor and struck her cheek. "You stupid bitch! Stay inside!"

Topo was there to help her up. "If you hurt her, the Boss will have your balls. She just wanted to see the rain."

"Why does she need to see the rain? It's just rain, *güevón.* If she goes outside, someone might see her and recognize her from the news."

That had been precisely the point—to let anyone who might have the warehouse under surveillance see that she was here. Delta Force usually handled hostage rescues, and there was no way they would charge in without knowing for certain that the hostages were here. Then again, the US wouldn't risk getting caught on Venezuelan soil.

There might not be a rescue.

Gabriela straightened her tunic, doing her best to seem unfazed, her cheek throbbing. "Thank you, Topo."

"I'm sorry, *Hermana.*"

She turned and faced Pitón. "I forgive you."

His face reddened, and he opened his mouth to speak.

Gabriela cut him off. "You treat me like a prisoner, but I

am no man's captive. I can do God's work, no matter where I am. There is no reason to behave like a guard dog. I would not try to escape and leave the hostages alone with you."

With that, she turned her back to him, determined to show him that he didn't scare her. Her words seemed to have had their desired effect. When she glanced back, Pitón stood there, his eyes burning not with lust, but with loathing.

She'd made an enemy of him. She'd dressed him down in front of the other men. He wasn't the kind of man to put up with that. He would want to get even.

But not today.

She made her way downstairs and sank down on her blankets, the throb in her cheek now a headache.

Dianne noticed first. "What happened?"

Gabriela touched her fingers to her cheek. "I stepped outside to see the rain. One of the men didn't like it. He dragged me inside and shoved me. I fell and hit my cheek on the floor."

Tim leaned in. "You're probably going to have a black eye. The bastards. Er... Sorry, Sister."

"Do not be sorry." Gabriela wished she had some ice. "God knows you are under great distress. Besides, I think you may be right. Some of them might be bastards."

She smiled at the shocked expressions on their faces. "Do you think I've never used profanity before?"

"What made you decide to be a nun?" Dianne asked.

Under Gordito's glowering watch, Gabriela told them the story—how she'd known from an early age that she wanted something different for herself, how she'd always loved church, how her priest had arranged for her to meet a religious sister one Sunday after Mass.

"Sister Benedicta invited me to visit her convent. I knew

from the moment I stepped inside and felt the peacefulness that this was the life I was seeking."

Gabriela had told the story a hundred times and knew she was convincing. She'd spent months preparing for this assignment. But there was one element of truth in it.

She'd been a restless teen and had, indeed, wanted more from life. She'd studied law enforcement, thinking she might be a detective or work for the FBI. But the Agency had recruited her after graduation, their interest piqued by her linguistic skills and her ties to Venezuela. She hadn't looked back.

"You're so young." Tim looked like he felt sorry for Gabriela. "Aren't you going to wish one day that you had a husband or children?"

How like a guy to think that all a woman needed to be happy was a guy.

"The world is full of children who need food, shelter, and love. Those are my children, and I love them all. I know my own mind. For me, there is no love like the love of God."

Dianne smiled, looked over at Tim. "Is that hard for your male ego?"

It was apparent the two had worked together for years and were good friends.

Tim shook his head, stretched out on his blanket. "It's just hard to understand. Sex is a basic human drive. I'm not sure how a person gives that up."

Gabriela loved sex. Not that she'd had many men. Her parents had been very strict when it came to boys. She'd had a serious boyfriend her last two years of college, but it hadn't lasted beyond graduation. Mitch had wanted a traditional marriage. She'd wanted a career. Dating had become tricky after she'd joined the Agency.

Even so, she was more old-fashioned than her friends.

She wasn't into casual sex or Tinder or online dating. Still, the idea of going without the possibility of sex for a year or more had been intimidating. To her surprise, she'd been so tired every night that she hadn't even thought about it.

Gabriela kept that to herself. "Do you want to hear what I miss most?"

Dianne and Tim nodded almost in unison.

"Blue jeans and rock music." What she wouldn't give for a classic rock station.

"Shut up, over there!" Gordito shouted in Spanish. "You talk too much."

Head still aching, Gabriela sat on her blanket, folded her hands, and closed her eyes, as if she were in prayer. During these silent periods, she rarely prayed. Instead, she used the time to get focused, to think.

Had anyone spotted her? Was the building under surveillance? Or had she gotten this black eye for no reason?

DYLAN FINISHED a quick-and-dirty workout of pushups, sit-ups, and squats and took a quick shower before sitting down to a breakfast burrito of powdered eggs, black beans, salsa, and potatoes. "Hey, man, you make a good burrito."

"Don't act so surprised." Segal had been on duty all night, and it was his turn to make the morning meal. "Tel Aviv has some of the best Mexican food in the world."

Jones was on duty at the window. "Come on, man. Tel Aviv?"

"Do you think all we Israelis eat is gefilte fish, latkes, and Chinese?" Segal sat down with his own plate. "Come taste for yourself."

Dylan took a sip of coffee. "Anything happening over there, brother?"

"Nah, man. They've changed the guards a couple times, but I haven't seen any of the hostages."

Last night, they'd broken out the thermal camera and done their best to peer through the windows. They hadn't found the hostages, but they had learned a couple of things. Though there were guards on the roof, no one was positioned on the two upper floors, which remained completely dark. More importantly, there'd been a faint light coming from the small basement windows.

Someone was down there.

While Segal took a quick shower, Dylan finished his breakfast, did the dishes, and then relieved Jones so he could grab a bite.

"I'm impressed," Jones called over to him. "These burritos are good, even with the powdered eggs. Don't tell Segal I said that."

Dylan chuckled. "And give him an even bigger head? No way."

"I heard that!" Segal yelled from the bathroom.

Then it was time for their check-in with Shields and Tower.

"We've run all the photos through face recognition and analyzed the footage from last night." The image of Shields on their laptop's monitor had frozen, but Dylan and the others could still hear her voice. "That's definitely Sister María Catalina and the man who abducted her—a well-known *sicario* known as Python—Pitón."

So, that's what the *hijoeputa* called himself.

Time to cut the head off that snake.

Shields went on. "There's an almost one hundred percent probability that the other hostages are there, too."

"Could the nun be colluding with Sánchez or the cartel?" Segal had gone on about that yesterday evening. "The guards didn't try to stop her when she walked outside."

Dylan found himself jumping once again to Sister María's defense. "You saw that son of a bitch drag her back inside, right? That's them trying to stop her."

"He did more than drag her inside." The frozen image of Shields vanished from the screen, replaced by a photo of the warehouse door. "We magnified the images you sent. Not only did Pitón drag her back inside, but he also knocked her to the floor."

Dylan leaned close to the screen, Jones and Segal doing the same. In the grainy shadows of the open doorway, he could just make out that bastard shoving Sister María. In the next image, she was flat on the concrete.

But Segal couldn't let it go. "Why didn't the other guards try to stop her?"

"Venezuela is a predominantly Catholic nation," Shields said. "These men might be uncomfortable treating a nun as a captive."

Dylan could understand that. "Yeah, man, nobody wants to mess with a nun."

Tower's voice came over the speakers. "There's more to it than that, but, yes, that's essentially it. She's been in communication with the Reverend Mother at the convent in Peru. Her captors allowed her to write a letter. Sánchez's men have made her their go-between. She's taking care of the hostages, and they've given her a little more freedom of movement. In this case, she crossed the line."

Dylan met Segal's gaze. "Satisfied?"

Segal waved off Dylan's question. "Sure."

Shields appeared again. "So far, I've counted fifteen

different men. I'll keep analyzing the photos as you send them and see if that changes."

With a full Cobra team of six, they could take fifteen guys with no problem.

"In the meantime, we need everything you can get us about the layout of the warehouse," Tower said. "I need to know every way in and out of the building."

"Want us to knock on the door and ask for a tour?" Jones joked.

"That wouldn't be my first choice." Tower didn't even grin.

Dylan had to bite back his own smile. "On it, boss. We'll set up our black-market stand today, let them get used to seeing us in the neighborhood, try to scope the place out, maybe get a game of *fútbol* going."

Tower acknowledged that with a single nod of the head. "The images you captured last night show a low level of light coming from the basement, probably from a battery-operated lantern of some kind. It's likely the hostages are there. We don't want to risk killing them with stray rounds, and we don't want these fuckers killing them when we start breaking down doors. Remember Sar-e Pol."

Sar-e Pol was a textbook example of a hostage rescue gone to hell. US special forces had moved in on an ISIS position where three Americans and one German were being held hostage. They hadn't known that a guard was positioned near the hostages with instructions to blow them all sky high in case of a rescue attempt. The moment US operators moved in, the guard had clacked off an S-vest, killing himself, two operators, and all of the hostages.

Of course, this wasn't Afghanistan, and these fuckers sure as hell weren't ISIS.

Tower glanced at his watch. "Unless something comes

up, our next check-in is at seventeen-hundred hours.
Thanks."

The screen went dark. The meeting was over.

$\sim$

GABRIELA MET Pitón's gaze without wavering. "What do you
want Ms. Connelly to do—bleed through her clothes? Do
you want to send her home in blood-stained trousers? What
about when my time comes? Is this what you'd want for
your mother or sister?"

Dianne had brought this up last night, and Gabriela had
seen an opportunity to get outside once again. She'd had
intensive HUMINT training—human intelligence—and
couldn't imagine Pitón or any of these men wanting to ask
on the streets about feminine hygiene products. If she could
persuade them to let her do it...

Pitón shifted uncomfortably, clearly not at ease with this
topic. "I don't know about such things. Tell her to use toilet
paper."

"You told me we didn't have much toilet paper. She
could go through most of a roll in a single day. After
a week—"

"Topo!" Pitón gestured for Topo to join them. "We need
some ... things for the women prisoners. I need you to go
and find ..."

Was it so hard to say?

"Tampons or pads," Gabriela finished for him.

Topo stared at Pitón in horror. "You want me to ask on
the street about ... those things? ¡Mierda!"

"I'm not going to do it." Pitón reached in his pocket, drew
out US dollars. "You go—and don't spend too much."

Topo stepped back, shook his head. "I can't—"

"Mary, Mother of God, give me patience!" Gabriela saw her chance. Maybe this time, someone on the street would recognize her. "If you two *brave* men are so afraid of pads and tampons, then take me with you, and I'll do it."

They stared at her, mouths open.

Pitón caught her chin between his fingers, turned her face to look at her bruised cheek. "What about your face?"

"You created that problem, not I."

Pitón stepped back, his expression shifting from anger to resignation. "Topo, take her with you. If she tries to run, shoot her. If she says anything she shouldn't, shoot her. If she gets away from you, I'll shoot you. Do you understand, *güevón*?"

Topo nodded, looking less than happy about the arrangement. "Don't run, *Hermana*. I don't want to shoot you."

"I won't run, Topo."

Topo reached inside his shirt and drew out the key that hung on a chain around his neck. He unlocked the main doors, and they walked out into the street, the sun warm on Gabriela's face, the air humid but fresh.

Topo pointed with a jerk of his head. "Those men are selling things."

Almost directly across the street, two men were doing a brisk business in black-market goods, their wares stacked behind them.

As she'd done last time, Gabriela turned her head to the left and to the right then looked upward, hoping to give anyone surveilling the place a good look at her face. "Let's go and see what they have."

Gabriela crossed the street and waited her turn, watching the men work. One, a tall, good-looking black man, kept track of the money, a pistol visible in the waistband of his jeans, while his partner, a man with a Cuban accent, negotiated with customers, his face turned away from her.

The first thing Gabriela noticed was how comparatively little these men were charging, not turning anyone away, but making sure that everyone was able to afford what they needed, whether they paid in bolivars, Colombian pesos, or US dollars. The mother who needed diapers and condoms, the grandmother who was desperate for corn flour, the boy sent for rice—no one left empty-handed.

Then the Cuban turned to her, met her gaze—and Gabriela's heart seemed to stop.

God, he was good-looking, his features a mix of European, Latin, and African, his lips full, his eyes a light shade of gray.

It took her a moment to realize he was speaking to her.

His gaze focused on her bruised cheek. "Is there something you need, *Hermana*?"

Somehow, she found the words. "*Tampones o toallas sanitarias, por favor.*" *Tampons or pads, please.*

"*Sí*, we have those, but not here." He turned to the man behind him, who hurried away. "I've sent my friend upstairs to get them."

"Gracias." Gabriela glanced back to find Topo standing a good five feet behind her, probably embarrassed.

"Is there anything else you need, *Hermana*?" the Cuban asked.

She'd just opened her mouth to answer, when the man leaned closer and whispered for her ears alone.

"We're here to free you and the other hostages, Sister," he said in perfect American English. "Don't be afraid."

Holy shit!

Adrenaline hit her bloodstream, but she kept her composure.

She pretended to examine a bag of coffee beans. "We're in the basement. They have seventeen men. There's an armed guard with us at all times. The stairway to the basement is to the right of the main doors. There's no other way out of that room. The windows are too high and barred. Topo, the man behind me with the glasses, has instructions to shoot if I say too much or try to run."

He looked behind her, saw Topo, then switched to Spanish. "The coffee beans are yours, *Hermana*. Will you pray for me?"

"Of course." Overwhelmed with relief, she made the sign of the cross. "May God bless you and keep you. In the name of the Father, the Son, and the Holy Spirit. Amen."

The other man, who must also have been a US operative, reappeared with a box of maxi pads and a box of tampons in his hands. "For you, *Hermana*."

She paid with the handful of dollar bills Topo had given her, the intensity in the man's gray eyes offering reassurance.

Not wanting to arouse suspicion, Gabriela hurried back to Topo, her hands full. "They gave me the coffee beans in exchange for a blessing. See? I told you I would not try to run away."

"Come. Pitón is getting impatient." Topo took the coffee beans from her and hurried her back to the warehouse.

4

D ylan worked with Jones to keep the merchandise moving, hungry, desperate people looking at them with hope in their eyes. He handed an older woman an extra bag of beans, wishing he could do more for her. "For you, *abuelita*."

"God bless you!"

When they'd sold through the stock they'd planned to sell today, he and Jones headed upstairs, both careful that they weren't followed. They didn't say a word in English until they were behind the locked door of their apartment.

"Holy shit, brother." Jones walked to the fridge, took out a bottle of water. "Can you believe that? She walked right up to us."

"I got it on camera," Segal said from across the room. "You spoke with her."

Dylan recounted his brief exchange with Sister María. "She told me the hostages are in the basement and that there's only one entrance—a flight of stairs to the right of the main doors. There's a guard with them at all times.

There are seventeen men in the warehouse, so we've missed two somehow."

The two men gaped at him.

Jones looked impressed. "She told you that? Smart nun."

Segal left the window, walked over to them, his gaze on Dylan. "You took a big risk by revealing us to her."

"Listen, man, I know it's not in the playbook, but I saw that bruise on her face and wanted her to know she's not alone."

In truth, Dylan had wanted to cross the street and put a bullet through Pitón's skull, but that would have to wait.

Segal swore in Hebrew. "Our security is more important than her morale. What if she tells the other hostages and someone overhears? What if one of them lets it slip?"

"Brother, you need a nap." Jones sank onto the sofa. "If she's smart enough to give us actionable intel, she's probably smart enough not to tell anyone we're coming."

"It's like she knew exactly what we need to know." This had to be the luckiest damned op of Dylan's career. "Let's get this information to Tower."

Five minutes later, they were in a video conference with Tower and Shields again.

It wasn't often Dylan saw Tower taken aback by news. "She told you all of that?"

"In one breath." Dylan respected the hell out of her.

Okay, so he also had a bit of a crush on her.

She's a nun, a virgin, a bride of Christ.

He'd always been an idiot when it came to women. That's why he chose to stay single.

"Was she alone?" Tower asked.

"No, the *sicario* with thick glasses was a few steps behind her, keeping an eye on her. She said he had orders to shoot if she ran or said too much."

"Why would they send her to do the shopping?" Segal asked.

"Oh, come on." Shields smiled. "That's easy. Do these guys seem like they'd feel comfortable asking other men for menstrual products?"

Now that Shields mentioned it, it *had* surprised Dylan when Sister María asked for pads or tampons. He'd never thought of nuns as having periods. He'd grown up thinking of them as holy figures who had more in common with the Blessed Virgin than they did with other women. But, of course, they must have periods like every other human female.

"Point taken." Tower read back what he had in his notes. "Is that everything?"

"Yes, sir. We ought to be able to move quickly now."

Tower nodded. "I'll bring Andris into the loop, and we'll start building the op. I want more information about the inside of the warehouse. There must be another way into that basement, something the good Sister hasn't seen. I'd like more information about those windows—how big they are, whether the bars are removable, and so on."

But Tower wasn't done. "Cruz, I'm looking at you now. Don't get too familiar with Sister María. If she starts buying something from you every day or spends too much time chatting with you, Sánchez's men are going to get suspicious. They're not idiots. They might move the hostages, and then we'll be starting from scratch. Don't tell her anything else. Understood?"

"Yes, sir."

"It's almost sixteen-hundred hours. There's no point in talking again in an hour. Let's check in tomorrow at oh-eight-hundred."

The meeting ended.

Jones chuckled, got to his feet. "He set you straight, brother."

"Yeah, well, I probably deserved it."

"He let you off easy." Segal stretched, grinned. "I'd have fired your ass."

"Hey, Segal, how do you say 'fuck off' in Hebrew?" Chuckling, Dylan walked to the window, took a seat, and began his watch.

GABRIELA WASHED the bowls that had held tonight's portion of beans and rice, ignoring Pitón's drunken ramblings, her mind on her brief conversation with the American spec ops guy.

We're here to free you and the other hostages, Sister. Don't be afraid.

She'd never been so happy to see US military personnel. At the same time, she'd been astounded. She knew what was at stake—not just her life and the life of the hostages, but the relationship between the US and Venezuela.

If US troops were discovered on the ground here...

She ought to have realized right away that they were spec ops. It wasn't just their physiques—all that muscle. It was also the neat haircuts, their awareness of their surroundings, the way they carried themselves with that hard edge one only saw in special operations guys. But the real giveaway ought to have been their low prices, as if the money weren't important.

The black market in Venezuela was ruthless.

The man she'd spoken to, the one with the gray eyes, had called her *Sister*. That meant the Agency hadn't broken her cover and she needed to remain Sister María Catalina.

The Agency must be trying to protect their string of assets, from the Reverend Mother Beatrice in Peru to Gabriela's contacts here. If it got out that the religious sister who was abducted with two US journalists was an Agency officer, the diplomatic fallout would be terrible—and good people would die.

"*Eh, Hermana!*" Pitón walked up behind her. "I asked if you're a virgin."

On her knees, she was vulnerable, so she stood. "What happened to make you so hateful? Pitón isn't your real name."

"He's Eduardo," one of the men called out.

Sniggers.

"You were baptized Eduardo, but now you go by Pitón. Why?" She willed compassion to fill her voice, not the loathing she felt for him. "Who was so cruel to you, Eduardo?"

He grabbed her by the arm, ducked down until his face was inches from hers, his breath reeking of alcohol, his skin unwashed, his fingers biting into her arm. "You need to speak to me with more respect."

She looked him straight in the eyes. "If you want my respect, you must earn it."

"I could order my men to rape you. By the time we're all done, not even Christ would want you."

She refused to show fear. "Nothing you can do to me could change who I am. My strength comes from God. Besides, your boss would punish you."

"You're drunk, Pitón." Topo moved cautiously toward them, clearly afraid of the bigger man. "Leave her alone!"

Pitón released her, staggered back, drew his pistol—and waved it at Topo. "Shut up, you stupid—!"

BAM!

Gabriela gasped, watched in horror as Topo crumpled, blood bubbling from a bullet hole in his throat, his glasses flying.

"I didn't mean to shoot! The gun just went off!"

She ran to Topo's side but knew there was nothing she could do. She took his hand, gazed into his terrified eyes. She didn't care that she wasn't a priest or even truly a nun. He'd been shot trying to protect her. She would do all she could to ease his passing. "What is his real name?"

"Miguel!" someone shouted.

"Sor-ry!" He managed to croak.

"Don't be afraid, Miguel. You're in God's hands now." She began to pray. "Through the holy mysteries of our redemption, may Almighty God release you from all punishments in this life and in the life to come. May He open to you the gates of paradise and welcome you to ever-lasting joy."

Topo/Miguel seemed to relax—or maybe that was just blood loss.

With her free hand, she made the sign of the cross over him. "May God forgive you of your sins, in the name of the Father, and of the Son, and of the Holy Spirit."

He shuddered—and was gone.

Gabriela closed her eyes, fought to control her shock—and her rage.

Behind her, that *malparido* Pitón was doing damage control. "It was an accident. You all saw that. It was an accident."

Gabriela closed Topo's lifeless eyes, her gaze falling on a chain that had hung around his neck. The bullet had split it. Lying on the floor in a pool of blood was the key. She'd seen him use it to unlock the main doors.

Did she dare take it?

If they found the broken chain, they would suspect her, and then God only knew what they'd do. With Topo gone, Pitón would be more of a threat, and Gabriela didn't want to do anything to put the other hostages at risk. Then again, if she could get it to the guys across the street, they might all get out of this hell hole sooner.

Keeping her head bowed so her veil would conceal her actions, she took the chain and the key and slipped them both inside her tunic.

Then she crossed herself with a bloody hand and stood to face Pitón. "Someone needs to tell his family and call for a priest to—"

"¡*Cállate!*" *Shut up!* Pitón slipped his pistol back into his jeans. "We'll drive his body to the river. Find plastic bags or a tarp."

"Pitón, man, we don't have those things. We'll have to go find some tomorrow."

Gabriela spoke on impulse. "Those men who sold me the tampons also had plastic bags. You could try to find them. I saw them walk around the corner. They can't be far."

She was sure the spec ops guys would be watching, but getting Pitón to ask for their help wouldn't be easy. Getting close enough to hand them the key—that was going to take a miracle.

DYLAN STOOD with the others at the window, the lights in the apartment turned off. "What the fuck is going on in there?"

Jones had been on duty at the camera when the three of them heard what sounded like a gunshot. "They're opening the doors. I see Sister María."

Click. Click. Click.

Dylan moved into action, grabbing his SIG. "Segal, you take the camera. Jones and I will head down to the street and see if we can overhear anything and figure out what's going on. Jones, grab the soccer ball and some smokes."

Needing to look like smugglers, they tucked their firearms in their jeans and took the stairs as fast as they could, stepping into the warm, humid night. They sat on the stairs, ball between them, and lit up a cigarette.

"Did you see her ass?" Dylan wanted it to seem like they'd been sitting there for hours, just two guys shooting the shit.

The bastard called Pitón came around the corner, followed by two of his men.

Dylan didn't acknowledge him. They were strangers, after all.

Pitón stopped. "Were you selling things in the street today?"

Pitón had come looking for them?

"Is there something you need?" Dylan stood, handed the cigarette to Jones, who pretended to take a drag.

Neither of them smoked.

"Plastic bags, the big kind."

"*Sí*, we have those." Dylan gave Jones a nod, and Jones headed back up to the apartment.

"Cuban?" Pitón seemed to study Dylan.

Dylan nodded. "I came to support the Revolution."

"And get rich selling stuff on the black market." Pitón grinned, his expression telling Dylan that he could at least respect those motives.

Dylan smiled back. "That, too."

Jones must have taken the stairs two at a time, because he returned quickly, a box of black plastic bags in hand.

"How are you paying?"

Pitón drew a five-dollar bill out of his pocket. "Is this good?"

"*Sí, claro.*" *Of course.* Dylan grinned, took the money, while Jones handed the bastard his plastic bags. "Give him a cigarette, too. When you pay with US dollars, you get a bonus."

Pitón seemed pleased by that. "*Gracias, panas.*" *Thanks, buddies.*

We're not your buddies, you motherfucker.

Dylan watched him go, he and Jones staying on the steps until the cigarette burned itself to ash. Then they headed back inside, neither of them speaking until they were behind locked doors once again.

"What the fuck was that about?" Jones asked.

Combined with that gunshot, it seemed pretty clear to Dylan. "Anyone want to bet they're getting rid of a body?"

But whose body was it?

"You two need to see this."

Dylan walked through the dark apartment to the window, but the doors to the warehouse were closed again. "See what?"

Nothing was happening in the street below.

"This." Segal scrolled through images on the camera.

An image of Sister María peering out from the doorway, as if watching Pitón and his men. Sister María looking back over her shoulder.

"What is she doing—trying to escape?"

"No, man, watch." Segal had taken video of what came next.

Sister María stepped outside and all but ran into the street and dropped something in the middle of the road before hurrying back indoors.

"What the ...?" Dylan stared at the screen. "We better go see what she dropped."

"I'll go. I need some fresh air." Segal stood, tucked a weapon into his jeans, and grabbed an old-school iPod and some earphones.

Dylan and Jones watched through the window as Segal, head nodding along to his music, came around the corner and walked down the center of the darkened street.

"He'd better find it."

"He will."

Long minutes passed before Segal bent down, retrieved something, and slipped it into his pocket. Then he took off down the street again, probably planning to walk around the block. A few minutes later, the door opened, and he stepped inside.

"You're not going to believe this." He reached into his pocket and drew out a broken chain—and a key. "She left us a fucking key."

"A key to what?"

"I'm guessing she thought we'd be smart enough to figure that out."

They moved the camera gear away from the window and drew the curtains before turning on the light.

"It's covered in blood." Segal walked into the kitchen, washed it off in the sink.

Dylan followed him. "Could that be her blood?"

"She didn't look injured when she ran into the street."

Dylan took the chain while Segal washed his hands. The chain had been broken by force, the key large, the kind that opened a big deadbolt. "We need to check in, get all of this to Shields and Tower."

5

After she'd cleaned up the blood, a man they called El Cebo—Bait—brought Gabriela back down to the basement where Dianne and Tim were relieved to see her alive. While El Cebo told Gordito what had happened, she explained the situation to Dianne and Tim in whispers.

"Pitón accidentally shot and killed Topo when he tried to defend me."

"Dear God." Dianne took Gabriela's hand. "I thought they'd killed you."

"*¡Cállate!*" *Shut up!* Gordito looked angrier than usual and got in El Cebo's face, speaking in fast and furious Spanish. "Pitón is a stupid bastard. Why do all of you follow him? You're like sheep. You're cowards."

Gordito and Topo had been buddies.

El Cebo shrugged. "The boss put him in charge. They're taking Topo's body to the river now."

"*Mamagüevos!*" *Cocksuckers!*

Gordito shoved El Cebo aside and bolted up the stairs.

El Cebo stared after him then seemed to realize he was now in charge of the hostages. "No talking!"

Gabriela sat on her blanket, pretending to retreat into the solace of prayer, indistinct shouts coming from upstairs. She drew a breath, tried to let the stress of what she'd just witnessed drain from her. She and the hostages were safe.

They're going to come looking for that key.

Yes, but they wouldn't find it.

The guards had left her alone to clean up the blood while they'd moved the body. She'd seen her chance, so she'd taken it, running into the street, dropping the key and chain on the chance that the spec ops guys were watching.

What if they didn't see you? What if they don't find it? What if they find it but have no idea which doors it opens?

She refused to worry about it. If they *did* find it, it might make the rescue operation easier. If they didn't, they were no worse off. They had their own master key in the form of explosive breaching charges.

Gordito returned to his post, visibly enraged. Dianne and Tim settled down to sleep, so Gabriela did the same, worries gnawing at her. She knew when she heard the thunder of boots on the stairs that Pitón was coming for her.

The door burst open, and he appeared, rage on his face, two others following him through the door, El Cebo and another.

Pitón reached for Gabriela, jerked her to her feet. "Where is the key, you little whore?"

"What key?" She looked at him as if he were crazy, addressing him by his real name to take him down a notch. "You're still drunk, Eduardo."

"You took Topo's key to the front door while you were praying over him. It had to be you." He released her, stepped back, hate on his face. "Gordito, search her. Take off that ugly gray habit. Let's see what this bitch is hiding."

Gordito looked scandalized. "Pitón, man, she's a nun. If

you want to search her, you do it. I'm not going to touch her."

Pitón swore, reached over, ripped off Gabriela's veil and coif, her hair spilling around her face. He shook the fabric, threw it aside. "Where did you hide it?"

Tim stood and might have tried to stop Pitón had Gabriela not shaken her head.

"I am hiding nothing." She fought to stay calm. "All of you were standing right there, Eduardo. How could I possibly take anything? What would I do with it?"

If he got her naked, she was sure he wouldn't stop there.

Pitón untied her scapular, jerked it over her head, then started to untie the rope at her waist.

"Man, he wore that key around his neck." Gordito glared at Pitón with disgust. "Did you check the body before you threw him in the fucking river, *pendejo*?"

Pitón turned on Gordito. "Of course, they checked the body!"

Then he turned to a younger man whose name Gabriela didn't know. "You checked his body, right, *güevón*?"

The man's gaze dropped to his feet. "We searched his pockets."

"You searched his pockets?" Pitón let loose a string of profanity. "When I asked if you'd gotten his key, all you'd done is search his pockets?"

"*Sí*, Pitón. I'm sorry. I didn't know to check around his neck."

"Fucking idiot!"

Gordito seemed amused by all of this. "Relax, Pitón, you stupid fucker. That key is now in the river with poor Topo. We have others. Besides, how is this little nun going to get past me? Even if she had a key, she couldn't do anything with it. You'd better start worrying about what you're going to tell the Boss. Topo was his wife's nephew."

That was useful information.

"Shut the fuck up!" Pitón turned and stomped up the stairs, leaving stunned silence behind him, El Cebo and the other *sicario* following.

Gabriela let out a silent breath of relief.

She had gotten lucky this time.

Gordito shut the door, motioned toward Gabriela's veil, coif, and scapular. "You can put them on. Is it true that you prayed over Topo?"

"Yes." Gabriela slipped the scapular over her head, tied it in place. "He said he was sorry. I prayed to God to forgive him of his sins."

"You did that?" Gordito stared at her as if seeing her for the first time.

"Yes. I could not absolve him, but there was no one else. Pitón refused to call a priest, and Topo was so afraid. I didn't want him to die in fear. God will understand."

If she could feed the tension between Gordito and Pitón...

Some of the anger left Gordito's face. "Thank you, *Hermana*. Can I get you anything?"

Gabriela slipped the coif into place then reached for her veil. "A deck of cards? Something for the gringos to read? You know how dull things are down here, Gordito, because you are here with us."

"*Sí, Hermana*. I'll make it happen."

⁓

"I NEVER PLAYED SOCCER." Jones tossed the soccer ball to Dylan. "I only played football."

"I'll help you out." Segal settled in behind the camera. "You kick the *ball* with your *foot*. Got that? That's why the entire world, except for the US, calls it *foot*ball."

"You think you're funny, don't you, man?"

Dylan didn't join in the banter. He'd felt uneasy since last night when that gunshot had gone off. They'd watched as a body wrapped in plastic was carried onto the loading dock and dumped into a van. What the hell had happened over there?

He went over the plan. "We play for a while. You try to get the ball from me, and then I'll take it from you. That kind of thing. Then, when the time is right, I'll kick the ball into one of those window wells. If the guards raise their weapons, we stop, act surprised and friendly, and let them get it for us."

"Got it."

Last night, Segal had gone for another walk, this time making his way around the warehouse. He'd found a door that went downstairs, but it had clearly been in disuse for a while, the stairwell full of dirt and trash. There wasn't even a guard posted there—a sign perhaps that it was bricked up from the other side or inaccessible in some other way. Sister María had said there was only one entrance to the room where she and the others were being kept.

Now, it was up to Dylan and Jones to gather intel on those windows—if they could get close enough.

Dylan dropped the ball to the asphalt and dribbled it down the street. Jones came up beside him and almost tripped him trying to get the ball away.

Speaking Spanish now, Dylan ribbed him. "What was that, *pendejo*?"

Over on the loading dock, a couple of *sicarios* were watching, grins on their stupid faces.

Dylan and Jones grappled over the ball, Jones finally stealing it and dribbling it the other way. Dylan ran up beside him, stole the ball, and took off. Back and forth they went, working up a sweat in the hot sunshine, the guards shouting encouragement and laughing along with them.

Then Dylan saw his chance. He kicked the ball straight toward one of the basement windows. It rolled and sank into the window well.

Goal!

"*Mierda.*" *Shit.* Grinning and chuckling, he jogged toward the window. "Out of bounds. Sorry."

One of the *sicarios* by the main doors shouted for him to stop, but he pretended not to hear, bending over and reaching for the ball.

Iron bars bolted into concrete. Gaps not wide enough for a person to pass through. Windows made of single-pane glass.

There was no way anyone was going in or out of these windows.

"Hey, *güevón*, what are you doing?"

Dylan scooped up the ball and stood, putting a dumb smile on his face. "Just getting our ball, buddy."

They went back to playing, stealing the ball from one another until at least an hour had passed.

"You're getting better," Dylan said to Jones, still in Spanish. "Let's get something to eat, *pana.*"

They were due to check in with Tower and Shields.

This time, Andris was there.

Tower didn't like what Dylan had to say. "There's no way to get those bars off without risking injury to the hostages?"

"None, sir."

"What about additional entrances?" Andris asked.

"We've got the main doors and loading dock and then a side entrance. Anything else?"

"I circled the place last night," Segal said. "The only additional entrance I found is an unused door that goes down to the basement. The hinges have rusted, and there's a few years' worth of debris piled up in the stairwell—leaves, trash, mud."

Dylan offered his two cents. "We need to know that's not a dead-end before we try to get in that way. We don't want to blow the hinges only to walk into a brick wall."

Then Jones chimed in. "Why can't we just kill the guards and use the key? They've got at most six guys at the doors and two on the roof. If we use suppressors and move at night, we might be able to get inside without anyone knowing we're there."

Segal shook his head. "We'd have to neutralize all our targets at the same exact time, or someone will set off the alarm, giving them a chance to kill the hostages."

"Actually, it might be our best bet," Andris countered. "They won't take the sound of a key sliding into the lock as a threat. Is there any chance that they've changed the locks?"

"No way." Dylan was certain of it. "We've been watching round the clock."

"I'd sure like to know who they killed," Shields said. "If it was one of the journalists, we should know soon. The US government has asked for proof that the two journalists are alive to buy us some time."

"This is going to be a complicated operation." Andris didn't need to tell them that. "We've got forty-eight hours to get in there and get this job done. We'll be wheels up at zero-six-hundred hours tomorrow."

Hell, yeah.

Shit was about to get real.

❧

"WHAT SHOULD I DO NOW?" Gabriela pretended not to know she had a straight flush.

Somehow, Gordito had gotten them a deck of cards. Because a nun probably wouldn't have mastered poker, Gabriela had played ignorant, prompting Gordito, who'd gotten sick of watching her lose, to become her coach.

"Call it."

"I call." Gabriela set her cards down on the blanket.

Tim grinned. "That's the third hand you've won."

Gabriela translated this for Gordito, doing all she could to create a bond between him and his prisoners. "You're a good teacher."

"I used to play poker all the time."

"Don't tell me you gambled, Gordito?" She smiled.

He chuckled. "Are you trying to make me feel guilty, *Hermana*?"

"If guilt works, then..."

Gordito's phone buzzed, the smile leaving his face. He drew the phone out of his pocket and answered. "*Sí. Sí, Jefe.*" *Yes, boss.*

He ended the call, stood, his expression grave. "Hide the cards. Now!"

"We need to hide the cards," Gabriela told the others, gathering them up.

Heavy footfalls on the stairs.

By the time the door opened and Pitón walked in, the cards were tucked away in their box and hidden beneath Dianne's blanket.

Pitón dropped a copy of today's newspaper on Dianne's lap. "Have these two hold up the paper while I take a photo.

The bastards in Washington want proof that they're still alive before they release the money."

Then he noticed Gabriela. "Not you, whore. You stand over there. Nobody cares if you're alive, not even your God."

Gabriela stood, stepped away from Dianne and Tim, eager *not* to be in the photo. The last thing any of them needed was for her face to appear in US newspapers. People might recognize her.

She watched while Tim and Dianne held up the paper and looked into the camera on Gordito's cell phone.

Gordito took a couple of images then uploaded them to someone.

Was the person he'd called *Jefe* Luis Sánchez?

Gabriela wanted to get her hands on that phone.

Then Pitón was gone again, even Gordito looking relieved.

An hour later, one of the men shouted down to Gordito that the hostages' supper was ready. "Send up the nun to get it!"

"I'm going with you, Hermana. I don't trust that *malparido*."

Gabriela didn't have to ask which bastard Gordito meant. "Thank you, Gordito."

Gabriela climbed the stairs and crossed the space to fill bowls for herself and the others, Gordito staying by the top of the stairs.

"Why the fuck are you here and not down with the gringos?" Pitón was drunk again, the tension between him and Gordito sharp.

But Gordito didn't seem to be afraid of Pitón. "I'm here to make sure no one touches her."

"Who would want to touch her?" Pitón laughed. "I bet a

nun's pussy dries up. Is that what happens, *puta*? Does it dry up?"

Gabriela ignored him, filled three bowls with rice and beans, and tucked three bottles of water under her arm.

Pitón stepped into her path. "Or maybe it fills up with cobwebs and rats."

That brought snickers.

"Let her pass, Pitón, you *malparido*."

Pitón glowered at Gabriela but stepped back. "When we release the other hostages, I'll be free to do whatever I want with you."

Gabriela ignored him, made her way downstairs once more, Gordito and Pitón arguing, their shouts following her to the basement. Alone for just a moment, she tried to buoy their spirits. "The photos they took of you two today—that was proof of life. They said the US government demanded proof that you were alive before they would transfer your ransom money."

Gabriela knew that no ransom was on its way. This was just a stalling tactic, a way of buying time for the spec ops team. But she couldn't risk people's lives by telling Dianne and Tim that a rescue was imminent. They'd all seen the soccer ball hit the window this afternoon, but only Gabriela had recognized the man who'd retrieved it. She'd known it meant the operators were looking for weaknesses, searching for the best routes in and out of the warehouse.

"Do you really think they'll let us go?" Dianne asked.

"Yes. Do not despair." Gabriela took Dianne's hand, squeezed it. "Soon, you will be safely home again."

It was just a matter of days.

6

D ylan sat with Jones and Segal around the laptop for a briefing on the rescue plan with Tower, Shields, and Andris. But first, Tower shared some good news.

"The body they moved did *not* belong to the hostages. You've seen Sister María yourself, and the Pentagon received proof of life for the journalists today. They killed one of their own."

"Better that than a hostage."

"Save us effort."

But now it was time to get down to business.

Shields led off. "You're in a densely populated and mountainous area, so infil is going to be tricky. We'll do a HAHO insertion over the *Zona Militar*. Satellite images show no movement there for weeks now except at the small base on its northwest boundary. Under cover of darkness, it's unlikely anyone will spot our guys. But if people in surrounding towns see men in parachutes coming down, hopefully they'll assume it's Venezuelan forces."

Okay, Dylan was on board with that. High-altitude, high-open jumps—HAHO jumps—were intended for areas like this one, where the sound of a parachute opening might alert an enemy on the ground.

Tower took over. "The drop zone will be a narrow band of forest about three klicks east of your position. Team Two will pack their chutes and meet you at these coordinates. You'll be waiting there with the truck at oh-two-hundred hours. This time you'll be smuggling us."

Then it hit Dylan. "You're coming, too, boss?"

"Corbray and I will both be there. He's meeting us at the airport in Miami."

Dylan exchanged glances with Jones and Segal. This must be one hell of an important mission if they were both coming. It had been a long time since both Corbray and Tower had deployed with the team. The risk was obvious. They were the company's owners. If something went wrong and they were killed...

Andris went over the rescue. "Tower and Corbray will take positions at the window of your apartment where they can get a clear shot at the men on the rooftop. The rest of us will use the truck for cover or position ourselves around the corner. We'll be using night vision and suppressors."

Suppressors couldn't make a rifle silent, but people inside the warehouse shouldn't be able to hear the shots.

"It is paramount that all eight targets are neutralized at the same time so that no one raises the alarm," Tower said. "We don't want to give these bastards time to kill the hostages. You'll sight your targets and drop them on command."

"Got it."

"Understood."

"We'll make it happen."

"From there, it will be a pretty standard rescue, except that we hope to enter using the key Sister María so bravely provided rather than breaching charges. Hopefully, that will buy us some time."

Andris took it from there. He clicked the computer's trackpad, and a satellite image of the warehouse appeared on the screen. "Once inside, Cruz and Jones will head straight to the basement to free the hostages, while McManus, Segal, Isaksen, and I clear the building. Tower and Corbray will keep an eye on the street in case these bastards have backup. We are not taking prisoners. Am I understood?"

It was shoot to kill.

Dylan didn't have a problem with that. These bastards worked for a drug cartel and a corrupt government official who killed anyone who got in his way and who had chosen to abduct US citizens. There was a price to pay for that kind of shit.

"Once the hostages are free and the building is clear, we'll take the stairs up to the roof for exfil. A Sikorsky S-76B will drop out of the sky to ferry us to a US navy vessel sitting offshore in international waters. Tower and Corbray will meet us on the roof with the gear from the apartment."

With the broader plan outlined, they broke it down into small details.

Dylan, Jones, and Segal would sell off the rest of their black market wares this afternoon, including the beer and the *cocuy*, which they hoped to get into the hands of the bad guys.

Segal would stay at the apartment and maintain surveillance while Dylan and Jones drove to the drop zone to pick up Team Two. He would make sure to leave the window facing the warehouse open in preparation for Tower and Corbray so there would be no sound or movement to draw the guards' attention as they got into position.

Before firing shots, the men would break down all of the surveillance equipment and laptop and get it ready for Tower and Corbray to carry to the warehouse roof.

"Easy-peasy, huh, boys?" Shields smiled.

But Tower was dead serious. "I do not have to emphasize how critical it is that every step of the operation is carried out to perfection. You are the best of the best—elite warfighters with the skills to work privately. Your lives, the hostages' lives, and the future of US-Venezuelan relations depend on us getting this right."

When he put it that way...

"We'll see you all tonight," Tower said.

"Godspeed."

The screen went blank.

Dylan stood, stretched. "You heard the man. Let's make it happen."

They had a lot to get done between now and oh-two-hundred hours.

"No, *puta*, you stay up here tonight." Pitón was in a mean mood and drunk again, this time on *cocuy* he'd bought from the spec ops guys. "Gordito, you go be with the hostages."

Gabriela stood rooted to the spot, a bad feeling in her chest.

"I'm not leaving her with you, you drunk *maricón*. The boss will feed your balls to his dogs if you touch her."

"Shut up!" Pitón was apparently too drunk to care what his *jefe* would do. He drew his pistol and pointed it unsteadily at Gordito. "Get down there with the hostages, *mamagüevo*, or you'll take a swim with Topo."

Gordito drew his firearm, too, but walked backward

toward the stairs, his face dark with fury. "If anything happens to her, I'll kill—"

"She'll be fine." Pitón grinned. "Do you think I would hurt a nun?"

"I'm sorry, *Hermana*." Gordito disappeared down the stairs, leaving her with Pitón and a handful of his men.

Just great.

As she'd done before, she retreated into the role of a nun, feigning serenity. She looked for something to do, a way to occupy herself, but it was after midnight, supper long over, the dishes already washed and dried.

"Bring me that bottle, whore." Pitón pointed to the bottle of *cocuy* near his feet.

If she did as he asked, she would be in easy reaching distance.

She sat, tucking her legs beneath her. "No, Eduardo. You're drunk enough."

He stomped over to her and grabbed her by her hair, his hand fisting in her veil as he dragged her painfully to her feet. "How do you know when it's enough? You've never been drunk."

Snickers.

He forced her over to the bottle. "Pick it up."

She did as he demanded, handing him the liquor. "Drink your soul away, if you wish. It won't make you feel better about killing Topo."

Gasps.

He jerked the bottle from her hands and backhanded her, the blow splitting her lip, leaving her dazed. "Watch yourself, *Hermana*. You don't think I've killed women before?"

Gabriela licked the blood from her lip and willed herself

to meet his gaze. "I'm certain you've committed a great many mortal sins."

He raised the bottle to his lips, took a long drink. "Where's the music?"

Caballo Viejo, an old folk song, started playing over small, tinny speakers.

He sank into a lawn chair, pointed toward his feet. "You sit here."

She did as he demanded, turning her back to him.

Nearby, El Cebo and two others sat on their blankets playing poker, US dollar bills piled high in the center. Two others sat on the stairs that led to the loading dock playing a Venezuelan card game called *truco*. Another tried to change the music.

"Leave it alone!" Pitón shouted.

Gabriela spent the next hour or so as Pitón's servant, fetching him water, lighting his joint, bringing him food—and ignoring his filthy mouth and slurred words.

"I bet if you got laid, you'd give up the Church."

"Jesus can't do for you the things I can do."

"Have you ever sucked a man's dick? No, you probably haven't. Have you even seen a dick?"

Couldn't this *malparido* just pass out?

She hugged her knees to her chest, rested her chin on her knees, and pretended to sleep, her senses trained on the room around her.

The reek of alcohol, cigarettes, marijuana, and unwashed bodies. The *click* of a lighter. One of the men snoring.

How he could sleep with music blaring and the lights on—

The door opened, bringing her head up.

She caught a glimpse of men in battle gear and would

have thrown herself flat onto the floor if Pitón hadn't yanked her to her feet and forced her to run.

Behind her, the spec ops team opened fire.

Pop! Pop! Pop! Pop! Pop!

"One of the tangos has Sister María and is running toward the rear entrance."

What about Dianne and Tim?

Pitón pulled her down a hallway, his pistol drawn.

As soon as they were out of sight of the others, she let her rage out, drawing on her combatives training and hitting Pitón squarely in the gut with her elbow.

Taken by surprise, he grunted, doubled over.

"*Malparido!*" She laced her fingers together and struck him on the back of the neck then tried to kick the pistol from his hands. But her damned skirt was too narrow, stopping her and almost making her fall over.

Fury on his face, Pitón slammed her in the chest with his shoulder, forced her back against an iron pillar, and shoved the pistol against her cheek. "Do that again, *puta*, and I'll put a bullet through your brain!"

"You won't get away, Eduardo. They'll kill you. You should surrender."

"Shut up!" He dragged her around a corner, pushed open a side door, and ran outside, only to find the two men who'd been guarding it dead on the ground. "*Malparidos!*"

"You can't escape."

Panicked, he looked up and down the dark, silent street —then put the pistol to her head and used her as a shield as he made his way to a parked car. "If they try to stop me, you're dead."

Come on, guys! Stop this asshole!

And then he was there—a man in full combat dress and night vision goggles, his rifle raised and pointed straight at

Pitón. He moved forward with the grace of a predator, step by step. He shouted to Pitón in Spanish. "Let her go!"

Gabriela recognized his voice. It was the one who'd pretended to be Cuban. Swamped with relief, she almost smiled.

Pitón froze. He tightened his grip on Gabriela, one arm around her throat, the barrel of his pistol pressing painfully against her temple. "I'll kill her *right now* if you don't drop your rifle."

Gabriella spoke in English. "Pull the trigger."

THAT'S NOT what Dylan had expected Sister María to say, but he didn't need her encouragement. He exhaled —and fired.

Pop!

The bastard was dead before he hit the ground.

Dylan reached for his hand mic. "Cobra Actual, this is Cruz. The last tango is down. I've retrieved the hostage and am heading toward extract."

He jogged over to Sister María, still speaking Spanish. "Are you okay, *Hermana*?"

"*Sí.*" She wiped blood spatter off her cheek, her lip split and swollen. "Let's get out of here."

That sounded good to him. He didn't like being separated from the others. "Can you run? We need to get up to the roof."

"Yes. Where are the other hostages?"

He was touched by her selflessness. A lot of people in this situation would be concerned only with saving their own asses. But, of course, she was a nun. "They're already on the roof, waiting for a helicopter. Come. We must hurry."

They had run just a few feet when Dylan heard the roar of truck engines.

Tower's voice came over his earpiece. "Cruz, this is Cobra Actual. Take cover! You've got enemy QRF pushing your position, coming in fast from the north."

What the fuck?

He made a split-second decision. "This way, *Hermana.* More bad guys are coming to join the party."

They ducked inside the open doorway of an apartment building across from the warehouse. Dylan shut the door, watching through a window as three big troop transports rounded the corner and stopped in the middle of the street. "Get down!"

Dozens of armed men jumped to the ground and rushed into the warehouse.

Son of a bitch!

For an operation that couldn't go wrong, this was now an official clusterfuck.

"Cobra Actual, this is Cruz. We're pinned down across from the warehouse. There's no way for us to make extract. Twenty or so hostiles are inside the warehouse and headed your way."

"Copy that."

The rest of the bastards spread out, surrounding the warehouse. They weren't regular Venezuelan military.

Sister María looked out the window. "*Guachimanes*—the Watchmen, Luis Sánchez's private army. So now we're stuck here?"

She sounded more irritated than afraid.

"For now." Dylan could just see the roof of the warehouse, the Sikorsky appearing out of the night and coming in to land. "If they don't lift off quickly, they're going to come under fire."

Then he saw something that made his blood run cold.

Two of the men unloaded a crate from the back of the truck and opened it to reveal an RPG—a rocket-propelled grenade. The thing wasn't assembled yet, but when it was, it would shoot the helo out of the sky.

"Cobra Actual, this is Cruz. Hostiles on the ground have an RPG. I say again, they have an RPG. You need to get airborne—*now*."

"*¡Mierda!*" Sister María whispered. *Shit.*

Dylan couldn't blame her for the lapse. If that helicopter didn't lift off fast, they would watch while the others were blown to bits. If he'd been by himself, he'd have opened fire and done his best to take out the men in the street.

Tower seemed to read his mind. "Cruz, this is Cobra Actual. Do not engage! We'll get you out some other way."

"Copy that."

Sister María looked up at him, her face hidden in the shadows. "Is the helicopter going to make it?"

"I don't know."

The Sikorsky lifted off and nosed into the wind, the team now returning fire.

Ratatat! Ratatat! Ratatat!

In the street not twenty feet away from him, idiots who'd clearly never used an RPG before almost had it figured out.

"*¡Puñeta! Fuck!*

Seconds felt like hours as the helicopter passed overhead, picked up speed, and disappeared.

Godspeed.

Dylan let out a relieved breath.

Then ...

A baby's cry. Worried voices.

"What's happening?"

"That's gunfire. Someone was shooting."

"Stay down, *mi amor*!"

The noise had awakened the neighbors, and it was only a matter of time before someone opened their apartment door and discovered them here.

"We need to hide!" Sister María whispered. "This way."

Weapon raised, Dylan followed her down a narrow hallway to a set of stairs that led down to a door with the word *Mantenimiento* — Maintenance — painted on it in large, black letters. The door was padlocked.

"Stand back." He kicked the door open then flicked on the light.

Electrical panels. Pipes. Emergency water shut-off. Janitorial supplies.

Dylan drew Sister María inside and closed the door behind them.

In his earpiece, Tower announced they were safely away.

"Cobra Actual, this is Cruz. Copy that. We've taken shelter in a basement. Will stay in touch via cell phone."

The team would soon be out of range of his radio.

"They made it?"

"Yes." Dylan saw relief on Sister María's face.

"Thank God." She glanced around. "Now what?"

"Now we survive."

7

This wasn't how Gabriela had expected the rescue to end. At least Dianne and Tim were on their way home again.

When she spoke next, it was in English. He'd spoken English to her before. He obviously knew she was from the US, even if he didn't know her real profession. "What's your name?"

"Dylan Cruz." He raised his night-vision goggles, which were fixed to his helmet, then took off his helmet and shucked off his backpack. "I've got a medic kit. It looks like someone roughed you up. Let's take care of it."

She touched fingers to her swollen lip. "The man you killed did that."

He pulled a kit out of his backpack. "I'm sorry you had to witness that."

He still believed she was a religious sister. Under these circumstances, would she be authorized to drop her cover? She had no idea. What had happened tonight wasn't in the playbook.

Better to keep your cover for now.

He reached for a metal folding chair and motioned for her to sit. "Sister."

"Don't apologize. You only did what he forced you to do."

"Live by the sword, die by the sword, right?" He handed her a moist wipe. "You've got his blood on your face."

"Thanks." She wiped first her face and then her hands, then handed him the wipe. "What branch of the military are you in?"

He tucked it into a plastic bag, "I used to be a SEAL. I was an assaulter with Blue Squadron, DEVGRU—what you civilians like to call Seal Team Six."

Gabriela was impressed. She knew what DEVGRU was.

"I work for a private military company now."

That explained the lack of a US flag or any other identifying feature on his uniform. It might also explain why the Agency hadn't told him and the others that she wasn't a religious sister. Her mission was classified as top secret. She doubted whether employees of a private company had top-secret security authorization.

"And your family is from Cuba?"

He grinned. "Puerto Rico."

That was intriguing. He faked the accent well.

He put on a pair of sterile gloves, tore open an antiseptic towelette, and knelt beside her chair, the warm, salty scent of his skin making her want to inhale—and reminding her that she hadn't had a shower in more than a week.

His gray eyes looked into hers. "This is probably going to sting."

She lifted her chin and tilted her head to make it easier for him, wincing at the burn as he cleaned the cut.

"I'm sorry, Sister."

"It's not your fault."

His expression darkened. "I wish I had some ice. It looks like he punched you."

"Backhanded." She winced again. "I baited Pitón about killing Topo, the man who was with me the day I met you."

"You *baited* him?" Dylan drew back, his lips curving into a smile that put butterflies in her belly. "You also got that key to us—and gave us intel that helped us speed up the rescue. You are one brave nun."

She couldn't help but smile. "Says the man who took out sixteen *sicarios* with just five other guys—and who saved my life with a single shot."

He rocked back and peeled the gloves off his hand, his grin fading. "I wish I'd gotten you on that chopper. I'm sorry. We thought all of the hostages were together in the basement."

"We were—until tonight. Pitón wanted... my company."

Dylan searched her face, his expression worried. "If he ... *hurt* you ..."

Gabriela shook her head, touched by Dylan's concern. "He wanted to, but his boss threatened to kill him if he touched me. Mostly, I had to listen to his filthy mouth."

Dylan's brow furrowed. "Will I go to hell if I say I'm glad he's dead?"

She smiled. "I think God understands your relief that an evil man can no longer cause harm. Besides, who told you to pull the trigger?"

He stood, glanced at his watch. "It's almost oh-three-hundred. We can't leave until those guys clear out. We might as well get some sleep."

"And then what?" She hoped he had a plan to get home.

"As soon as they're gone, we move out."

"You can't go anywhere dressed like that." She motioned to his body armor and combat fatigues. "You'll be safer on your own. Just put me on a bus back to the mission in El Vigía—"

"No way." He put the medic kit back into his backpack. "Our orders directly from the Pentagon were to get you safely back to the US. I can't leave you behind."

"The *Pentagon*?" That was ... interesting.

Was the Agency recalling her? It must be if they wanted her back in the US. But why would they want her to come home when she hadn't yet gotten proof that Luis Sánchez was working with the Andes Cartel?

God, she wished she had some way to contact them.

"Are you hungry? I've got some emergency rations."

"Save them." She stood, smoothed her sadly wrinkled skirts. "What I really want is a shower."

"We'll have to work on that." He took another folding chair and propped it at an angle beneath the doorknob, bracing the door shut. "That won't keep anyone out for long, but it will give me time to react."

He carried his backpack, rifle, and helmet to the corner and sat with his back against the wall. "Come. I've got an emergency blanket. It should keep you warm."

Adrenaline giving way to exhaustion, she sat an arm's length from him, knowing that no religious sister would put herself physically close to a man. "Thanks."

He unfolded the crinkly silver emergency blanket and handed it to her. "You can sit closer and use my lap for a pillow. I promise I won't bite."

"Thanks, but I can't. It wouldn't be right."

She wrapped herself in the blanket, lay down with her head resting on her arm—and in the next breath was sound asleep.

～

DYLAN WATCHED SISTER MARÍA SLEEP, a strange sense of protectiveness swelling in his chest. Long, dark lashes rested against her bruised cheek, her veil revealing thick, dark hair, her small hand tucked beneath her chin.

She must have been exhausted to fall asleep so quickly. Or maybe the blow that had split her lip had given her a concussion. He would have to watch her.

What could he have done differently to prevent this? How could he have gotten her to the helicopter? She should be on a Navy vessel, sleeping in a warm bunk, not huddled with him in a dank basement.

He ran the last few minutes of the rescue through his mind—the rush into the basement, blowing away the lone guard, freeing the other hostages, seeing that Sister Maria wasn't there. He'd heard Segal say that one of the *sicarios* was running and had taken her with him. He'd run upstairs and onto the street, trying to cut the bastard off.

It had worked, but the lost time had cost them. Even if they had run like hell and made it into the building, there was no guarantee they'd have made it to the rooftop far enough ahead of the enemy forces to make it onto the helicopter. And if that helo hadn't lifted off when it had, they might all have been killed.

No, there wasn't anything he could have done differently. But now her life was in his hands.

Pull the trigger.

That wasn't what he'd expected her to say. There'd been no fear on her face, only deep trust in him and a sharp determination to survive.

He wouldn't let her down.

He set the alarm on his watch, closed his eyes, let himself drift.

The vibration from his watch brought him wide awake.

It was oh-five-hundred. Outside, the streets were quiet once more.

Had the bastards moved on?

Sister Maria slept still, her lips slightly parted, her face relaxed.

He hated to wake her, but they needed to get out of here before someone discovered them. "Sister, wake up. It's time to go."

Her eyes flew open, and she sat bolt upright. "What...?"

"Easy, Sister. It's okay. We just need to get out of here before someone finds us."

She nodded, straightened her veil, pulling herself together faster than he had expected. "I'm ready."

"I'm not." He stood, stretched, reached for his rifle. "I'm going to head up and take a look, make sure those bastards ... er... are gone. Sorry, Sister."

He needed to clean up his mouth.

"Please, don't worry about it. If you apologize every time you swear, I have a feeling you'll be apologizing all the time."

He couldn't help but grin. "You're probably right about that. Stay here. Don't come out no matter what you hear, okay?"

She met his gaze, nodded. "I understand."

He moved the chair, opened the door, and moved silently up the stairs and down the hallway to look outside.

The street was quiet with just early morning traffic. There was no sign of enemy forces. The body of the man he'd killed was gone.

The coast was clear—for now.

In the apartments around them, people were waking, getting ready for their day.

He needed to get Sister María far away from here.

He returned to the basement to find her on her feet and waiting for him. "The streets are clear."

"What are you going to do with your gear? You can't go out like that."

No, he couldn't.

He unstrapped his chest rig and body armor and dropped them to the floor and then unbuttoned his ACU shirt, stripping down to his T-shirt. "How is that?"

She looked him over. "Lots of guys wear camo, so I suppose the pants are fine."

He shoved his military gear into his backpack.

"If they search you, they'll find that stuff."

"That's a risk I have to take." He broke down his M4 and crammed it inside the backpack, too.

"We have one advantage," Sister Maria said. "They don't know we're still here in Venezuela. They think everyone was on that helicopter. They won't be looking for us."

He didn't want to scare her, but he was pretty certain there'd been witnesses to last night's drama in the street. "Let's hope not."

He checked his pistol and slid it into its concealed holster inside his pocket.

Somewhere above them, a door opened and closed.

"Time to go." He led her up the stairs and out into the cool of morning, guiding her around the corner and away from the warehouse.

"Where are we going exactly?" she whispered.

"Colombia."

Luis Rafael Sánchez Mantilla wanted someone to pay. He got up from his chair by the pool and walked back toward the veranda to pour himself a drink, phone to his ear. "How did the fucking gringos know where the hostages were? Someone in my organization betrayed me."

Luis had gotten the humiliating news first thing this morning and had shouted himself hoarse, cursing at the inept bastards who worked for him. He'd been bested by US commandos, who had invaded his country, killed his men, and escaped with his hostages while their government pretended to negotiate a ransom.

Malparidos! Mamagüevos! Bastards! Cocksuckers!

Ten million US dollars gone and shit on his face.

The president, his cocksucker of a brother-in-law, would hear of this, and he would laugh at Luis. He would call him stupid for taking hostages and trying to squeeze the US government. But this wasn't Luis' fault. He was surrounded by fucking idiots.

"There are some who saw the nun, *Jefe*. Pitón let her go outside. People saw her buying things at a market and recognized her."

What had Pitón been thinking when he'd abducted the Sister in the first place? That hadn't been part of the plan. Then the stupid bastard had let her walk in the streets?

If Pitón weren't already dead, Luis would've had him torn to pieces.

"But there is more, Don Luis."

"Out with it, Mono." Luis held his phone against his ear with his shoulder and poured himself a glass of whiskey.

"Pitón's body was found in the street, not in the warehouse. Some people who live nearby saw him running away with the nun. A commando chased him and killed him just before we arrived. Thanks to us, the soldier didn't make it back inside the warehouse. He didn't make it onto that helicopter. He took the nun and hid in one of the buildings."

Luis set the bottle aside, drink forgotten. "Are you certain?"

"*Sí, Jefe*. We searched the building and found a door to the maintenance room that had been broken open. There was no one there, but he is here in the city somewhere."

This...

This changed everything.

If Luis could capture this bastard, if he could prove that the US had operatives on Venezuelan soil....

His brother-in-law would be indebted to him for giving him the biggest public-relations coup of his time in office. Luis would demand an important ministerial appointment or a military rank as his reward for turning the soldier over for interrogation.

Of course, Luis would take his pound of flesh from this commando bastard first.

"Is the nun still with him?" She might be easier to identify.

"No one saw them leave the building, so we cannot be sure."

"Who knows about this?"

"About the commando? No one outside of your *Guachimanes*, Jefe."

"Keep this secret for now. Put police checkpoints on all the roads in and out of the city. Search every taxi, bus, and car that tries to leave. Cover the airport in Caracas, too."

"*Sí, Jefe*." There was hesitation in Mono's voice. "No one saw his face."

There were days when Luis wondered if he was the only one in his operation with a fucking brain. "He's a gringo. Check everyone's identification. He won't have an ID card, or, if he does, it will be fake. He probably won't speak Spanish. Detain any man traveling alone with a nun. Bring any gringos you find to me."

"What about the nun?"

Luis wondered if she would try to protect the gringo out of gratitude for rescuing her. "When you find her, bring her here. And, Mono, she must not be harmed. We have no quarrel with her. I'll see her returned safely to the mission."

"*Sí, Jefe.*"

8

I t was more difficult making their way through the city than Gabriela had imagined. The streets were crawling with *Guachimanes*, recognizable by their black uniforms and their rifles. It didn't take CIA training to figure out that someone had witnessed the fight in the street last night. Sánchez knew they were here.

The rumble of a truck engine.

Dylan drew her into an alley, the two of them ducking down behind a large steel trash bin. The truck, another troop transport, stopped at the corner, a dozen men leaping to the ground, their boots echoing up and down the street.

"It's getting too hot out here." Dylan had his pistol in hand. "We need to get off the street, *Hermana*."

They spoke only Spanish, as the sound of English would make them stand out.

"That's not going to be easy."

They had skirted the edge of town to get here, sticking mostly to stretches of park and forest, trying to reach the Carretera Panamericana—the Panamerican Highway—that would take them to Colombia. But this part of town was mostly apartment buildings.

The thud of heavy boots on asphalt grew closer.

"Hide in the trash bin, Sister. Quickly! I'll give you a boost."

She grabbed the edges of the heavy steel container, strong hands lifting her from behind, steadying her as she hoisted herself over the top and dropped into a waist-deep sea of garbage. The reek was awful—rotten fish, dog poop, cigarettes. Still, she didn't complain. She'd take bad smells over being caught any day.

Dylan dropped his pack over the edge and climbed in beside her, throwing a piece of discarded plastic over her, closing the lid, and retreating behind several full garbage bags. "Stay hidden no matter what happens. Don't worry about the rats."

"Rats?" She couldn't see in the dark, but she could hear them. "Shit!"

Boots. Men's voices.

Lying in the putrid darkness, she heard Dylan check his pistol, and her pulse picked up. She fought her fear, focused on listening.

"Perez, check behind the trash bin."

Perez, whoever he was, would surely look inside the bin, too. Had they hidden themselves well enough?

Footsteps drew near, stopped.

Then a shaft of daylight spilled in—and Gabriela's heart seemed to stop.

"*Dios mío*, it stinks!" The lid closed again, footsteps heading the other way now.

"Easy, *Hermana*." Dylan's voice was a reassuring whisper. "He's leaving."

They waited for what felt like an eternity before Dylan got to his feet and lifted the lid to peek outside.

"They're gone." He shouldered his pack, opened the bin, and climbed out, reaching back to help Gabriela. "We need to find somewhere to—"

"*Señor. Hermana.*" A boy who couldn't have been more than seven or eight years old motioned to them from a back door down the alley. "*¡Vengan! Los soldados los están buscando. Mi madre puede esconderlos.*" Come! Soldiers are looking for you. My mother can hide you.

Dylan cursed under his breath, hiding his pistol with his body until it was back in its holster. "Hey, friend." Dylan walked closer. "Is your mother here?"

A window just above Gabriela went up, and a woman with short hair stuck her head out, an angry expression on her face. She let loose on Dylan, scolding him in angry Spanish. "Why are you hiding this poor Sister in the garbage, you idiot? Quit talking, and come inside before someone recognizes her!"

"*Dylan.*" Gabriela whispered his name in warning, doing her best in the few seconds she had to rein in her adrenaline and assess the situation.

There was surely a reward for Dylan's capture. For families facing hardship, that money would be hard to turn down. Was this a trap?

It was the boy's guileless eyes that convinced her, soft brown eyes that held no hint of deception.

She looked up at the woman in the window. "*Gracias, señora.*"

Thank you, ma'am.

Dylan held the door for Gabriela, the child looking up at her as if she were a saint come to life.

She smiled. "What is your name?"

"Yadiel."

"Thank you for finding us, Yadiel."

The boy gave her a shy smile that put dimples in his cheeks.

Yadiel's mother hurried past them to close and lock the door. "I saw you jump into the garbage from my window. Those soldiers are searching for a man traveling with a nun. I recognized your face from the television, *Hermana*. Yadiel, close the curtains. I don't want anyone to see our guests."

"This is dangerous for you, ma'am." Dylan clearly had the same fear that Gabriela did. "If those men find out we were here—"

"Those devils." The woman's face twisted with anger. "You don't have to tell me that. They killed my husband eighteen months ago."

Gabriela crossed herself. "I'm so sorry. May God grant his soul repose."

Grief flashed in the woman's eyes and disappeared again. "I'm Laura. Let's see what we can do to keep the same thing from happening to you."

WHILE SISTER MARÍA spoke with Laura and Yadiel, Dylan memorized the location of doors and windows in case they needed to get out in a hurry, his gaze taking in the details of Laura's apartment. The tidy kitchen. A framed photo of a dark-haired man sitting beside a tiny sculpture of the Virgin Mary. The crucifix on the wall. A row of worn shoes on a mat by the front door.

"I don't have much to eat, but what I have I'm happy to

share." Laura gestured to the round kitchen table. "Please sit. Can I make you some tea? I don't have coffee."

"That's very kind of you, but I know how hard it is to find food." Sister María sat at the table. "I wouldn't want to deprive you or your son of—"

"It would be a blessing to me to help you, *Hermana*."

"You've already done that."

Dylan positioned himself in the doorway to the kitchen where he could keep an eye on both entrances. He didn't want to disrespect Laura by doubting her. Still, he needed to ask. "Why did you help us? If they discover what you've done, you and your son could pay the price."

Laura's expression sharpened. She set a kettle of water on the stove to boil, the silence stretching. "We have already paid the price. We went to a protest about the food shortages. The Guachimanes fired into the crowd, killing people who just wanted to feed their families. My husband died on the street in front of us."

"I'm so sorry." Sister María beat Dylan to offering condolences, empathy shining in those sweet brown eyes. "Would you like for me to pray for him?"

The anger on Laura's face transformed into grief. "You would do that?"

"Of course."

Laura led her to the living room with the photo of her husband and lit a small votive candle. "He was a good husband and father. He was a school teacher. He voted for the president. He believed they would make life better for all of us."

"He's not the only one who believed that." Sister María said gently.

She knelt, crossed herself, then folded her hands and began to pray in silence, her face luminous. When she had finished, she asked Laura if she would like to pray the *Ave Maria* with her. Laura knelt beside her, drew Yadiel against her, tears trickling down her cheeks, and joined Sister María. Dylan found himself praying along, the words he'd memorized as a child coming without effort.

When the prayer was over, Laura wiped her tears away. "*Gracias, Hermana.*"

In the kitchen, the kettle whistled.

They drank cups of hot tea together, Laura reminiscing about her husband and happier days.

Yadiel wrinkled his nose, his gaze on Sister María. "Why do you smell so bad, *Hermana*?"

"Yadiel!" Clearly embarrassed, Laura apologized. "How could you say such a thing? She had to hide in the garbage. That's why. I'm so sorry, *Hermana*."

"There's no need to apologize. You're right, Yadiel. I do smell bad. I haven't been able to wash for a week, and I had to hide in the trash."

Laura stood. "Come, *Hermana*. You can take a hot shower here."

Sister María looked at her with longing on her face. "That's very kind of you. Are you sure?"

"Of course! This way." Laura led Sister María toward the back of the house, little Yadiel tagging along behind. "We do at least have hot water and soap."

Dylan peeked out at the street from behind the curtains, saw the men in black uniforms piling back into the truck.

This had been a close call, and it wasn't likely to get easier. The Colombian border was only a twelve-hour drive away. At this rate, it would take them till Christmas to get there.

You should have gotten her onto the damned helo.

"Is it true what they're saying?" Laura stood behind him. "Are you a US soldier?"

Dylan wrestled with how to answer. Yadiel wasn't with her, so he decided to tell her the truth. "No, I'm not a soldier. I used to be in the US Navy. Now I work for a private military company. I came with others to rescue the hostages, and one of the *sicarios* tried to run off with Sister María. He pointed a gun at her head."

"Is he the one who hurt her? Her face is bruised—and her lip."

"Yes."

"Did you kill him?"

"Yes, I did."

"Good."

"Not good enough. I wasn't able to get Sister María onto the helicopter. I need to get her out of the country."

Laura crossed her arms over her chest. "That's not going to be easy. Everyone is searching for a man traveling with a nun. Her picture is everywhere."

Dylan had been afraid of this. "Is there any way that we could buy some clothing from you—something Sister María can wear that will help her to blend in. I can pay you. She's too easy to identify in that habit."

Laura nodded. "Yes, I can help you with that, but there's no need to pay me."

"How about a bag of coffee beans?" He'd saved two, along with some Cuban cigarettes, for his Tía Julia back home in Arecibo.

For the first time in the hour since he'd met her, Laura smiled.

～

IT FELT SO good to be clean, hot water, soap, and shampoo washing away some of the stress and exhaustion of the past week.

Gabriela combed her wet hair and studied her reflection in the mirror. The bruises on her cheek were darker now, her lip still a little swollen. There was a bruise on her right breast, too. She didn't know where she'd gotten that—probably from Pitón slamming her in the chest with his shoulder.

She hadn't seen her naked body much over the past couple of years, so it felt strange to stand there in privacy, not as the pious Sister María, but as Gabriela.

She dried her hair as best she could with the towel then reached for her plain bra, panties, and dirty, stinking habit, reluctant to put them on again.

A knock at the door.

"*Hermana*, I have laid out some clean clothes for you to wear. We don't think it's safe for you to be seen in your habit. You're too recognizable. I will leave you in peace to dress. If these don't fit, we'll find something else, but I think you're close to my size."

They were right about wearing her habit. The garments had protected her so far, but now they made her stand out.

Relieved, Gabriela wrapped the towel around herself and opened the door to find jeans and a yellow V-neck T-shirt emblazoned with a hot-pink poppy sitting on the bed beside a pair of pastel pink bikini-style panties and a black one-size-fits-all sports bra.

She hurried over to the bed, unable to keep from smiling as she ran her fingers over the faded, butter-soft denim. God, how she had missed jeans!

She dropped the towel, stepped into the panties, and reached for the jeans. Laura was shorter than she was and very slender, but Gabriela had probably lost ten pounds during her time at the Mission. The jeans fit like a glove.

She drew the sports bra over her head and then the T-shirt. And for a moment, she stood there, savoring the feel of wearing normal clothes again.

"*Hermana*, do they fit?"

"Yes, Laura, and thank you very much!" Gabriela gathered her dirty habit, panties, and bra, and bundled them into the towel, not sure what else to do with them.

She opened the bedroom door to find Laura standing there.

The woman's face lit up. "You're such a pretty girl. I'm surprised you had the chance to become a nun."

"That's very kind of you, Laura, but external beauty is fleeting." Still, Gabriela couldn't help but smile. "Thank you for lending me these clothes. I'm not sure when I'll be able to bring them back to you."

Probably never.

"Don't worry about that. Just make it to safety." Laura took Gabriela's filthy habit and underthings. "I'll wash these and save them."

"It's better for you to burn them. I don't want the Guachimanes to find you with them." Then she held out her rosary. "This is for you."

Laura stared at her in amazement. "I can't take it."

"You'll be helping to protect me. I've prayed countless times with this, so I hope it will bless you and Yadiel."

Then, over Laura's shoulder, Gabriela saw him.

Dylan stood down the hallway, leaning against the wall, arms crossed over his chest, his gaze moving over her, raw male hunger on his face.

Gabriela's belly fluttered, an emotion she hadn't felt in months stirring inside her—desire.

Dylan seemed to catch himself. He stood upright and looked away. "No one will think you're a nun now."

Gabriela had to hold back a laugh. "Let us hope not."

Laura invited Dylan to shower, too, an offer he couldn't refuse.

"I saw the way he looked at you," Laura said after Dylan had left the room. "Are you sure you're safe with him?"

Laura might do better to ask whether Dylan was safe with *her*, though the fact that she was working and maintaining her cover meant she couldn't jump his bones. "Yes, I'm sure. He has been most respectful. But I *do* feel naked without my veil."

It was the truth. She'd worn a veil for more than a year.

Laura gave her a sympathetic smile. "It's only for a short time. But what will you do? These mercenaries are everywhere. There are roadblocks on all the highways leaving the city. If they stop you, you'll have to show your ID, and then they'll have you."

That was going to be a problem.

"I don't have my ID. The people who abducted me didn't think to let me run inside to get it."

Laura studied her for a long moment. "I know a man who makes good fake IDs. He might be able to connect you with smugglers going to Colombia—if that's where you're going. But there's a reward for the two of you. I'm not sure you can trust anybody out there, not with people as desperate as they are."

"We trusted you." All the same, Gabriela would rather take her chances on the streets. With her training—and Dylan's—they stood a good chance of making it to the border on their own. But she couldn't say that. "Thank you, Laura. You have helped us today beyond all hope. Tell Señor

Cruz what you told me. He is the expert on such things. He'll know if it's too risky."

Then Dylan was there, his T-shirt stretched over his chest, his pecs visible through the white fabric, his short dark hair damp. "If what's too risky?"

9

"That must be the place." Sister María of the Very Tight Jeans pointed with a nod of her head toward the second-to-last house on the street. "Remember, you're my step-brother, and you're rescuing me from an abusive boyfriend.

"*Sí, claro.*" *Yes, of course.*

This had been Sister María's idea—and Dylan was impressed. In two flat minutes, she'd put the whole story together in micro-detail. The abusive ex-boyfriend. The need to get to Colombia, where Dylan, who'd come from Cuba with his poor departed father, had a construction job. The thugs that had stolen her ID card.

She'd suggested they use her birth name, which he already knew from the initial mission briefing, and combine it with Rojas, the last name that was on his fake ID. "That way, we can be relatives—siblings, spouses, whatever we need to be."

Dylan couldn't have done a better job himself. But he had to ask. "Won't you be breaking your vows to lie like this?"

"I vowed poverty, chastity, and obedience. Lying might be a sin, but God understands our circumstances."

Jesus, Dylan hoped so. He'd been uncomfortably horny since the moment Sister María had stepped out of the bedroom, those jeans and that T-shirt revealing all of the delicious curves that her shapeless gray habit had concealed.

She didn't just have a beautiful face and the heart of a saint. She had a body, too—full breasts, a slender waist, a sweet ass that filled out those jeans like...

Stop, cabrón. *She's a nun.*

Yeah, Dylan was going to hell.

If they hadn't been trying to escape a bunch of murdering assholes, he might have beat one out in the shower just to get the urge out of his system. But he hadn't wanted to get caught holding his dick instead of a weapon in case trouble came knocking, so he'd scrubbed off the sweat and grime and had gotten back to the job.

He needed to get Sister María back to the US. He couldn't afford distractions.

"You do the talking," she said. "I should seem afraid."

They walked up to the house, and Dylan knocked, his gaze shifting to the street around them, where kids kicked a soccer ball and adults sat on porches enjoying the sunset, not a Guachimán in sight.

The door opened to reveal a young man in jeans and a black tank top, tattoos on his forearms. "Yeah?"

"We need an ID. A friend sent us to you."

The man's gaze moved over Sister María in a way that put Dylan on edge. "Fifty US dollars."

Knowing he needed to haggle, Dylan made a counter-offer, pointing to the pack of cigarettes rolled into his T-shirt sleeve. "How about forty dollars and this unopened pack of Cuban smokes—Cohibas."

"Deal." The man grinned, stepped aside. "Come in."

He shut the door behind them, his gaze still on Sister María. "What do you need?"

Dylan poured out their story in all of its tragic detail. "I'm taking my sister, Gabriela, to Colombia with me to get her away from the bastard, but those guys who stole her handbag took her driver's license with it. We'll never make it past all these fucking roadblocks without it. What the hell is going on out there anyway?"

Sister María stayed silent, her gaze downcast, her dark hair spilling like a veil over her face, an air of vulnerability around her that hadn't been there before.

The man frowned, seeming to notice her bruises for the first time. "Why don't you just kill that son of a bitch? The fucker deserves it."

"As far as I know, that's still illegal." Dylan grinned.

The man, who said his name was Ender, laughed. "Too bad, eh? Let me get my wife. She can fix up your sister's face, and I'll make her an ID so perfect that even SEBIN wouldn't know the difference."

He shouted for his wife, asked her to bring her makeup kit. "Andrea used to work in a salon before it closed. Now she cuts hair in the neighborhood."

Andrea was a tall, full-figured goddess of a woman, her dark braids piled high on her head and wrapped with a bright red scarf. She examined Sister María's face. "Oh, what bastard did this to you? He should have his balls cut off."

Sister María gave her a shy smile, as if this sounded like a good idea to her.

Well, if she ever gave up being a nun, she could become an actress.

"I hope the son of a whore pays for this." Andrea went to work with concealer, cooing to Sister María as she made the bruise on her face disappear and hid her split lip with lipstick. "You look as beautiful as you ever did."

Sister María smiled. "Thank you, Andrea."

Ender led them to his basement, where he had a little shop set up with a scanner, a camera, a backdrop, and a fancy laminator. "Put that blouse on over your shirt. You don't want the ID to show the exact clothes you're wearing today."

Dylan had to give the man credit. He knew his business.

Sister María slipped into a white blouse, buttoned it, and then stood in front of the backdrop.

Click. Click. Click.

Then Ender went to work, hip hop playing in the background.

Sister María slipped out of the blouse, came to stand beside Dylan.

"How do you feel?" He touched her arm, a gesture of brotherly concern that he instantly regretted, the heat that arced between them, taking him by surprise.

She stiffened, clearly not prepared for physical contact. "I'm okay. Just a headache."

Ender turned to them, handed Dylan the ID. "See? What did I tell you? Perfect."

Dylan studied it. "I'm impressed."

He handed it to Sister María then pulled the cash from his pocket and the cigarettes from his sleeve. He had already taken the payment out of his backpack, not wanting to give anyone a glimpse of the money, gear, and ammo inside.

Ender took his payment, sniffed the cigarettes, and gave Dylan a homie handshake. "Thanks, man. Safe travels."

IT WAS TOO late to catch a bus to San Cristóbal, where they would stop before heading toward the Colombian border, so their priority after Gabriela's fake ID was finding something to eat and a place to spend the night. They walked toward the downtown area with its upscale restaurants, the night warm with just a hint of a breeze. It might have been pleasant—if they hadn't been running from bad guys, and if signs of hardship weren't visible everywhere.

People crowding around black-market stands. Families digging through garbage for food. Armed vigilantes, called *tupas*, standing on the street corners with weapons.

Despite all of that, Gabriela hadn't felt this free since the day she'd taken the veil.

Dylan's voice interrupted her thoughts. "You're smiling."

"I've missed wearing jeans."

"They look good on you. I ... uh ... didn't mean any disrespect by that, Sister."

She couldn't help but laugh. "No insult taken."

Dylan was doing his best to hide his reaction to seeing her in regular clothes. It was endearing, and it might have amused her more if she weren't fighting her own battle.

When they'd been running from the bad guys, she hadn't had time to appreciate how freaking *hot* he was. But now that they were just two people walking down the street, she couldn't seem to ignore the pull between them.

Everything about him turned her on. His dark, smooth voice. The muscles beneath his T-shirt. Those biceps. His smile. Those gray eyes and long eyelashes. That square jaw with its growth of stubble. His lips. Even the way he moved —graceful, masculine, sure of himself. Then again, he'd served as an elite SEAL and had mastered using his body in ways most men never would.

Damn.

It was best not to think about his body. She was clearly drowning in pheromones and suffering from toxic levels of chastity. But she couldn't do anything about that now, not if the Agency expected her to maintain her cover.

"Over there." She pointed with a nod of her head toward a restaurant across the street. "It's going to be expensive. Many of the restaurants in the city have shut down. Those that are open are expensive."

"Don't worry about the cost. I've got money."

They crossed the street. Dylan opened the restaurant door for her and followed her inside. The mingled scent of spices and roasting meat hit Gabriela in the stomach, almost making her moan. She hadn't eaten in almost twenty-four hours.

A hostess in big hair and makeup walked over, her lips flattening into a line of disapproval at their casual attire.

Dylan slipped her a twenty. "Sorry about the clothes. Our luggage got lost on our flight back from Paris."

She accepted the money, tucked it away. "How awful."

"A quiet table for me and my lady, please."

She led them to a table in the corner that faced onto the street and left them with menus, her attitude toward them transformed. "I hope they find your luggage."

Dylan sat with his back to the wall, which was Gabriela's instinct also, as it would enable her to see everyone who entered the restaurant.

"Order whatever you want," he said. "I know you must be hungry."

She perused the menu, her stomach growling audibly. Arepas prepared a half dozen mouth-watering ways. Steak with sautéed mushrooms. Roast chicken with new potatoes. Hearty *pasticho*, the Venezuelan lasagna her grandmother had once made.

She was almost too hungry to make up her mind. "It all looks so good."

You're supposed to be a religious sister, and gluttony is still a sin.

She settled on the *pasticho* and a glass of wine, while Dylan ordered an appetizer of arepas, steak, and a beer.

The drinks arrived quickly.

Dylan raised his glass. "*Salud.*"

"*Salud.*" She allowed herself only a sip, knowing that, without food in her stomach, the alcohol would go straight to her head and make her say something stupid, something about how sexy he was and how she wasn't really a Sister and how she wasn't into casual sex but she'd be willing to make an exception for him.

Dylan took a sip of his beer, seemed to study her. "You are not at all what I expected, Gabriela."

The sound of him saying her real name sent a shiver through her.

"How is that?"

"You swear more than I thought you would."

She winced at her lapses. "Ah. Yes. Sorry."

"It doesn't bother me." He leaned closer, lowered his voice. "Tonight, you became exactly what those people expected you to be—shy and afraid. You could be an actress. And the information you fed me, the way you got that key to us—it was like having someone on the inside. I couldn't have handled it better if I'd been a hostage."

"You couldn't." She smiled at his surprised reaction, her words a little prick to his ego. "They would have suspected you—the big, strong military man. That's the thing about being a religious sister. People are hardwired to trust us. Even though I stand out in my habit, I also move below most people's notice in a way you never could."

"Devious." He leaned back in his chair, his gaze still locked with hers, a grin spreading over his handsome face. "I like it."

DYLAN COULDN'T HELP but watch as Sister María took her first bite of her dinner. Her eyes closed, and she moaned, a soft, feminine sound of satisfaction that stirred him in all the wrong ways, making his blood run hot.

She chewed, swallowed, then dabbed her lips with her napkin. "It's been so long since I've had *pasticho*. My Abuelita Isabel used to make it when I came to visit. She's gone now."

Grief flitted like a shadow through her eyes, there and gone in an instant.

"I'm sorry." Dylan almost reached out to take her hand but stopped himself. He picked up his fork and knife and cut into his steak. "What did she think of your becoming a nun?"

Sister María smiled. "My abuelita was a good Catholic. She made sure I knew how to pray the Rosary when I was little. She would have been proud."

The conversation drifted as they ate, the two of them careful to keep their voices down. The work she'd done at the Mission. The desperation so many Venezuelans faced when it came to finding food. The lack of the most basic medicines.

Dylan couldn't take his gaze off her—those big eyes, the slight flush in her cheeks from the wine, those sweet lips, the tilt of her head when she smiled, the soft purr of her voice. And then he had to ask. "What made you give up everything? What made you decide to be a nun?"

She took a sip of her wine. "Why did you choose to do what you do?"

He grinned, amused that she'd flipped the question on him. "I've always been a strong, physical guy. I can do things other men can't do. I guess I wanted to make a difference."

"It was much the same for me. I saw a chance to do a job most people can't imagine doing."

"But you had to give up so much."

One slender eyebrow arched. "And you didn't?"

"I'm free to dress how I like, go where I choose, take lovers, raise a family, quit my job, start something new."

"Yet, here you are in San Antonio, risking your life, doing your duty."

She had a point.

Dylan was about to say so when movement near the front door caught his gaze. The hostess was blocking a woman who'd come in from the street, a child in her arms.

"No, please!" The woman tried to sidestep the hostess, then raised her voice. "Leftovers for my child? Anything? Please! He's hungry."

Voices stilled, heads turning.

Sister María's fork stopped halfway to her mouth, a stricken look on her face. She set her fork down. "*Madre de Dios.*"

Dylan realized what she was about to do and caught her wrist before she could stand. "Don't draw attention to yourself. Wait. You should finish your supper. You need to eat, too, build up your strength. You've been through an ordeal."

Her gaze met his, distress in her eyes. "I couldn't possibly eat more. The rest of the arepas—we'll get a box for them, too."

Dylan knew there was no changing her mind. He took the last swig of his beer, ate his last bite of steak, and motioned for the server. "Can we get a couple of boxes and the check, please?"

"*Sí, señor.*"

He paid in cash, called up the location of the hotel he'd booked on his phone, and they walked out together, Dylan's gaze moving surreptitiously over the other patrons to see if anyone was watching them.

Out on the street, Sister María craned her head, looking for the mother. "There."

The woman sat against a wall fifty meters ahead of them, her child in her lap.

Sister María walked over to her, knelt beside her. "I've got some pasticho here and some arepas for you and your little boy."

"*¡Gracias!*" The woman took the boxes, sniffed, smiled. She began to eat, feeding small bites to her child. "God bless you."

Down the street, a group of five young men had taken notice, either of Sister María or the food, and started walking their way.

Dylan sensed their aggression, their desire to fight. He took Sister María's hand. "We need to go—now."

She spotted them. "*Sí, claro.*" Yes, of course.

Dylan led her across the street. "Don't hurry, and don't look back over your shoulder. When the fighting starts, you do exactly as I tell you. Do you understand?"

"What about you?"

"I'll be fine."

Footsteps.

They reached the other side of the street.

"South." Dylan turned left, heading toward their hotel, footsteps telling him the men were almost on top of them.

To their right was the recessed entrance to an apartment building.

Dylan saw his chance. Without warning, he pushed Sister María into the recess. "Stay here, back to the wall."

Then he turned to face their pursuers, doing his best to remember his Venezuelan slang. "*¿Que hay, mis panas?*" *What's up, friends?*

10

Gabriela counted five assailants—all fighting-age males, two holding knives. "*Mierda.*" *Shit.*

"We're not your buddies," said one in a black Caracas Football Club T-shirt. "What's in the backpack, *guevón*? Hand it over."

Oh, man, these guys were stupid. Dylan had served with DEVGRU. He was among the best of the best. Couldn't they see that he was an experienced fighter? She thought about warning them but knew she couldn't afford to distract Dylan. Besides, sometimes people needed to learn the hard way.

"Want it?" Dylan's weight shifted, his knees bending slightly, a subtle change in posture that told Gabriela he wasn't going to cooperate. "Come and get it."

Her pulse spiked, her body responding on instinct, muscle memory resurrecting her training.

He doesn't need your help. Besides, religious sisters don't fight.

The men moved in on Dylan, the grins on their faces telling Gabriela that they were confident they'd come out on top.

Idiotas.

The Caracas FC fan lunged, somehow slamming his face into Dylan's boot, his knife clattering to the ground along with the rest of him.

"Stop before you regret it," Dylan warned the others.

"*¡Mamagüevo!*" A second man ran at Dylan and ended up gasping and cradling his balls on the concrete.

Enraged, the others moved in all at once, fury on their faces.

Dylan made it look easy. He grabbed one attacker, slammed the guy's face into his knee, then threw him aside in time to punch another in the jaw.

That guy staggered but didn't fall. He came back for more, swiping at Dylan with a knife while the third tried to kick Dylan's legs out from under him.

Dylan sidestepped the blade, caught the kicker's leg, and flipped him onto his back. That left only the man with the knife standing.

Rage and fear on his face, he swiped at Dylan once again.

Dylan stepped easily out of the way, then caught the bastard's wrist, wrenched the knife from his grip, and in a single, smooth move, had one arm around the man's throat, blade pressed against his carotid. "Stop fucking around and go home before someone gets hurt. You hear me?"

Gabriela couldn't see the man's face, but she could hear the fear in his voice.

"*Sí. Sí.*"

Then she saw it as if it were happening in slow motion—the man in the Caracas FC T-shirt lifting his head, his fingers curling around the handle of his knife, his body lunging upright as he drove the blade toward the back of Dylan's knee.

Gabriela reacted on instinct, knocking him flat with a scissor kick to the chin.

Still holding a knife at the other guy's throat, Dylan gaped at her, astonishment on his face. "What the...?"

That's when the adrenaline hit.

He'd seen.

Shit.

How was she going to explain what she'd done?

Dylan gave the man he was restraining a hard shove. "I don't want to see your face again."

The man stumbled, looked at his injured buddies, and ran off, leaving them to bleed on the sidewalk and make their way home.

But now a crowd had begun to gather, people staring in silence.

Dylan took hold of Gabriela's arm. "We need to get out of here—now."

Stepping over the prostrate bodies of the men whose asses Dylan had just kicked, they headed down the street, people making way for them, giving them a wide berth.

They'd gone maybe two blocks when the National Police rushed by them, sirens blaring, probably headed toward the scene of the fight. On their tail was a pickup truck full of armed *Guachimanes*.

Gabriela walked faster. "How far away is our hotel? If witnesses share our description or tell the police which way we went..."

"It's a mile and a half away. We take a right up here."

Gabriela stopped, looked at the map app on his phone. "We'll go faster this way."

She led Dylan through an alley and then into a heavily wooded park, only too aware that they weren't safe here either. Gangs, drug dealers, prostitutes—they kept to these shadows, guarding their territories, suspicious of strangers.

Four women stood beneath a tree smoking. A group of three young men stopped kicking a ball to watch as they passed. An old man swayed on his feet on the path ahead of them, half-empty bottle in hand.

"I'm not sure this shortcut was such a great idea," Dylan said for her ears alone.

"Just walk like you belong here. Let all that operator testosterone show."

"Operator testosterone?"

"See that bridge?"

"The one with the armed guys blocking it?"

"We need to get across it."

"I knew you were going to say that."

"Just follow my lead."

"Sure, *Sister*."

Dylan was onto her. But what else could she have done? She couldn't let them hamstring him.

As they drew closer to the bridge, she slipped her arm around Dylan's waist, felt him tense at her touch. "Put your arm around me. You're my lover."

The contact was electric. But she didn't have time to think about that.

She started talking about the imaginary time her mother had caught the two of them stealing cigarettes as teenagers, willing herself to relax and laugh. "I thought my mother was going to turn us over to the police herself."

Dylan chuckled convincingly. "It's a good thing you're such a clever liar."

Yeah, he was onto her.

She shifted her attention to the men on the bridge, who watched them approach. She'd spent endless months in the role of a religious sister, suppressing her sexuality. It felt strange—and exhilarating—to flip the switch in the opposite direction. She hit them with everything she had, looking from man to man, giving them a sexy smile, speaking in a purr. "*Caballeros.*"

Gentlemen.

Like the idiots they were, they returned her greeting, looked her up and down, smiled—and moved aside.

DYLAN WATCHED GABRIELA WORK, saw the effect she had on the men—an effect to which he was not immune even though he knew it was an act. Was she DEA? CIA?

¡Puñeta! Fuck.

Why had it taken that scissor kick for him to see the truth? Why hadn't he realized she was an operative? How many nuns could deliver actionable intel? Or steal a key from kidnappers? Or stare down the barrel of Dylan's rifle without fear?

Pull the trigger.

She must think he was a fucking idiot.

Hey, man, the truth hurts.

Oh, she was good, everything about her screaming sex. It rolled off her like a drug, like a spell, the men forgetting they were guarding the bridge, their gazes moving over her, lust on their stupid faces.

"*Hola, mamacita.*" *Hello, sexy mama.*

"*Oye, jeva.*" *Hey, girlfriend.*

The bridge wasn't wide, forcing Dylan to take his arm from around her shoulder so they could walk single file. If these bastards decided to fight him, he'd have no choice but to draw his pistol and open fire. Thankfully, they seemed to have forgotten everything but Gabriela and her lethal curves.

Had her hips moved like that under her habit?

Quit looking at her ass.

A muscle-bound idiot with an AK stepped into her path, smiled down at her, gestured to Dylan. "If you get tired of that one, you know where to find me."

Dylan glared at the bastard.

She smiled, lowered her voice as if sharing a secret. "Don't let him hear you say that. He gets fucking angry when he's jealous."

So, now she was even using Dylan's responses to flesh out her little performance.

The man stepped aside, giving Dylan space.

Gabriela took Dylan's hand as they reached the other side, awareness once again zinging through him at her touch. She looked back over her shoulder, giving the men on the bridge one last brilliant smile. *"Buenas noches."* *Good night.*

They left the wooded area, emerging onto a major thoroughfare hedged by tall buildings, no sign of the police anywhere.

"The hotel is there."

"I see it." He drew his hand away, fighting to quash his irritation with himself—and with her.

She must have had a reason for keeping up the nun ruse and not telling him the truth. She had her mission parameters just like he did. It wasn't personal.

You're just pissed off that she played you.

He didn't like being deceived.

Dylan had only met one person with her skillset, and that was Holly Andris, a former Agency officer who now worked for Cobra, often alongside her husband, Nick

Andris. Holly had used her physical beauty and brains to get close to men—and sometimes women—who were deemed a threat to the homeland to set them up for surveillance. If Gabriela was as good as Holly, she would know every thought in his head and every damned emotion he felt.

At least now you know what you're dealing with, cabrón.

In a way, it was a relief.

Sister María of the Innocent Eyes was defenseless.

Gabriela? Not so much.

They crossed the street, Dylan keeping an eye out for police, *Guachimanes,* or anyone who might have followed them from the park.

Hotel Euro was twenty-one stories tall with security at the door. They checked in, Dylan giving the woman at the front desk the same story about their bags being lost on a flight back from Paris, while Gabriela stood close beside him like any happy newlywed, playing her part, the floral scent of her hair teasing him.

"We should call your mamá and let her know we made it."

Dylan nodded. "Don't let me forget. She'll worry."

"Here are your key cards, Mr. and Mrs. Rojas." A woman in heavy makeup handed them to Dylan. "Your WiFi password is written on the back. I'll let you know when your bags arrive. Enjoy your stay."

They walked to the elevator, stepped inside, neither of them speaking because of the likelihood of surveillance.

Their room was on the ninth floor on the corner and overlooking the street. It gave them quick access to the stairwell as well as a view of what was happening below. The only downside was the single king-sized bed.

Dylan let the weight of the backpack slide from his

shoulders to the floor. "You can have the bed. I'll take the floor. I'm going to lay in some supplies."

He went down to the concierge desk and bought some basics at ridiculous prices—toothbrushes, toothpaste, a brush for her hair. Back in the room, he found Gabriela checking for listening devices.

She put the cushions back on the chairs. "I think we're clear."

He dropped the small bag of supplies on the bed. "Okay, Sister María Cuss-A-Lot—or is it Our Lady of Krav Maga? Or maybe Saint María of the Tinder Date? Who the *hell* are you, and what are you doing in Venezuela?"

GABRIELA HADN'T EXPECTED anger from Dylan and was surprised to find that it stung. She did her best not to react. "Our Lady of Krav Maga—I like that."

He crossed his arms over his chest, his jaw set. "Answer the question."

"I'm Gabriela Marquez. That is truly my name. I'm here on an undercover assignment for the Agency. I can't tell you more than that."

"Okay, Gabriela. Why didn't you drop the act and tell me the truth last night?"

Gabriela couldn't understand this reaction. "Why does it matter? You thought you were rescuing a helpless religious sister, and you just found out that I'm not so helpless after all. I just saved your leg—and maybe your life."

The glare in his eyes softened slightly. "I'm grateful for that, but I *don't* like being deceived."

"That wasn't my decision." She sat on the bed, exhaustion getting hold of her. "When you introduced yourself, it was clear you didn't know I was an undercover officer. I took that to mean that I had to maintain my cover. I figured they were scrambling to protect assets and my family here in Venezuela. I certainly didn't do it to trick you. Like you, I have to follow orders."

The hard line of his jaw relaxed, and he uncrossed his arms. "So, you were just keeping to your mission parameters."

She nodded. "As it is, I might catch hell when I get back for giving myself away. I couldn't let that *malparido* stab you in the back of the knee."

"Not if you wanted to get out of here. Nice scissor kick, by the way. Yes, I saw it. I looked just in time to see."

"Thanks. I'm out of practice. I haven't been able to work out."

"No, I suppose not." He drew out his smartphone. "I need to check in, see if I can reach Cobra."

He disappeared into the bathroom and closed the door, leaving Gabriela to surf news channels looking for anything about the hostage rescue or the fight.

God, what a mess.

If that bastard Pitón hadn't dragged her away, she'd have been on that helicopter, and she and Dylan would be eating bad food on a US Navy ship somewhere in the middle of the Caribbean. Instead, she was stuck in a hotel room in San Antonio de Los Altos with a surly former SEAL a risky day's journey from the Colombian border, her mission unfinished.

And then on the screen, she saw herself.

Damn.

"The National Police tonight are asking for the public's help in locating a nun who was abducted from a Catholic mission in El Vigía early this week. Police believe she was abducted by a foreign national, possibly an agent of the United States. The suspect is believed to be armed and extremely dangerous. Anyone who has seen the young Sister is asked to call the National Police immediately."

Gabriela was glad that they still believed she was a religious sister. She was also grateful that they didn't have a photo or a description of Dylan. Unless they connected the Cobra operatives with the guys selling black market goods —and they might eventually—they would also have no idea that he spoke fluent Spanish or that he could fake a solid Cuban accent. They probably thought they were looking for a white guy.

She and Dylan could use that to their advantage.

As for Gabriela, sooner or later someone would recognize her. She needed sunglasses, a baseball cap, maybe some hair color. If she bleached her hair blond, she might be unrecognizable. Make-up, too, would help—anything to make her look less like the woman beneath that veil.

From the bathroom came the sound of Dylan's voice.

She wished she could speak to her superiors, explain what had happened. She supposed she'd have plenty of time for that during the debriefing once she got back to Langley. In the meantime, her objectives were clear.

Work with Dylan to stay alive—and get out of Venezuela.

He stepped out of the bathroom, a troubled frown on his face. "I spoke with my boss. Venezuela closed its borders, even the maritime borders."

"That's not good."

"Oh, and you can relax. The Agency shared the basics about you with Cobra. You were at the Mission to gather intel about Luis Sánchez and his ties to the Andes Cartel."

She was surprised the Agency had shared that much.

Dylan must have top-secret clearance after all. It was a relief. "Yeah, well, being abducted put a premature end to that operation. What's the plan?"

"There is no plan—yet." He lifted the backpack, set it down on the table, and opened it. "It's a sensitive situation. We've been ordered to stay put for the next twenty-four to forty-eight hours while things cool down, and Cobra and the Pentagon pull something together."

That wasn't what Gabriela had expected, but it made sense. "Okay, but please don't sleep on the floor. It's a king-sized bed. I trust you to keep your hands to yourself—especially now that you know I can kick your butt."

"You?" A dark brow arched, but he grinned. "Kick *my* butt? Not a chance."

As Gabriela brushed her teeth and got ready for bed, mind and body aching from fatigue, she had to admit to herself that there were worse scenarios than being stuck in a hotel room with a sexy operator.

11

Dylan stood looking out the window at the city lights and the street below. He couldn't tell from here that the country was in dire economic straits or that there were people down there who were starving.

Behind him, the bathroom door opened.

He glanced over his shoulder, saw Gabriela kneel next to the bed. "That wasn't an act, huh? You're religious in real life?"

He immediately regretted his tone of voice.

You're a dick.

Her gaze met his. "You respected Sister María for her faith, but you doubt mine? That's funny. I pray, if that's what you're asking, and I hope that God hears me."

He turned back to the window, gave her privacy, her prayer silent.

The bed creaked as Gabriela, done praying, crawled beneath the covers.

"You could have escaped those bastards on your own. When you brought that key out to us, you could have run off, but you went back inside. Why?"

"They had two US citizens, good people who were terrified. I was able to use my position as a religious sister to make their lives a little easier. I got them blankets, regular meals, water for drinking and washing. I couldn't just abandon them."

"You guilt-tripped the kidnappers into taking better care of them?" He could imagine that.

"More or less." The sheets rustled. "Do we have to talk about this now? I haven't gotten a full night's sleep since this began. I'm so tired I can barely think."

"That bastard I shot, the one who hit you—you could have taken him yourself."

"I tried. I'm out of practice, and the skirt was too narrow. I couldn't manage a good... kick." Her words trailed off, became a yawn. "He had a firearm. I didn't. I decided not to get shot on the way to my rescue."

That made sense to Dylan. "Smart."

"I'm glad you approve." Her tone of voice said she didn't give a damn what he thought. "If you've got an extra firearm, I want it."

It went without saying that an Agency officer could shoot.

"I've got a spare Glock you can carry."

"Perfect."

"Good work today, by the way—saving my leg, finding that shortcut, getting us across the bridge. You had those bastards wrapped around your finger."

"It's their balls—men's balls make them stupid."

"I can't argue with that." Especially given his response.

Gabriela had been through an ordeal and had done all she could to protect the other hostages, putting their safety ahead of her own, aiding Cobra's mission. She'd also done her part to help with the rescue and to get the two of them safely to the hotel tonight, stopping that bastard from hamstringing him, taking them on that shortcut.

So, why was he behaving like an asshole?

She had violated his trust. She had *lied* to him. Yeah, she'd had good reason, but that didn't change the fact that she wasn't who he'd thought she was.

Get over it, cabrón. *Your anger isn't about her at all. It's about Valeria.*

The truth of that sank in, stirring emotions he'd thought he'd left behind—hurt, grief, anger. He'd trusted Valeria, and she'd brought his world crashing down.

Fuck Valeria.

He shouldn't give her any space in his head or waste another moment thinking about her. She didn't deserve it.

Just like Gabriela doesn't deserve your attitude.

An apology on his tongue, Dylan turned to find her sound asleep, dark lashes against her cheeks, one hand tucked beneath her chin, her breathing deep and slow. Even with bruises on her face and a split lip, she was beautiful.

Jesus, he was an idiot.

Even knowing who and what she truly was, he couldn't help the sense of protectiveness that welled up inside him— or his attraction to her. It had been one thing to ignore his desire when he'd believed she was a nun. But now...

Now, nothing had changed. He needed to focus on his job. She was a client, and it was his mission to bring her to safety, not to get inside her. No, he wouldn't go to hell for having sex with her—not that he believed in hell—but he might lose his job. Worse, he might get distracted and get the two of them captured—or killed.

He brushed his teeth, made sure the door was locked, checked his pistol, and set the weapon on his nightstand.

Then he got into bed, staying on top of the covers and as far away from Gabriela as he could.

He closed his eyes, willed himself to relax, images of her drifting through his mind. Sister María telling him to pull the trigger. Gabriela stepping out of Laura's bedroom, all sweet curves in a T-shirt and jeans. Gabriela turning the men on that bridge inside out.

He fell asleep with a grin on his face.

GABRIELA ROLLED over in her sleep, snuggled against something warm, a pleasing scent filling her head, rousing her from sleep and arousing her at the same time.

She opened her eyes, saw that she lay with her face pressed against Dylan's side, her head tucked into his underarm. She scooted back, sat up, his scent still with her.

God, he smelled good—salt, skin, man.

He lay shirtless and still asleep, one arm stretched over his head, his face turned away from her, anatomy that had teased her through his T-shirt bared for her to appreciate. Pecs dusted with dark curls. Flat dark nipples. A furrow bisecting his six-pack. Obliques that disappeared beneath the waistband of his ACUs. A trail of curls that led straight to his zipper.

Damn.

It was like waking up next to a real, live Greek god. None of the other men she'd slept with had looked like this.

But there were scars, too. A deep groove in his left pec. A jagged line on one hip. A long surgical scar on the right side of his abdomen.

It was a record of combat, of battles fought and won, of survival.

"Like what you see?" His sleepy, deep voice startled her.

She did her best to cover her surprise—and embarrassment. "You've been hurt."

"It's part of the job description."

"How did you get that?" She fought back the urge to touch him, pointed to the groove in his pec.

He glanced down at his chest as if he couldn't quite remember what was there. "I was grazed by an AK round near Jalalabad."

"And that?"

"That came from the tip of an old bayonet." He spoke about it without swagger or machismo, just giving her the facts. "Some kid wanted to impress his daddy."

Gabriela didn't want to know what happened to the kid or his daddy. "And this?"

"I took a round to the gut a couple of years back on assignment in Mazar-e-Sharif. We were ambushed at the airport while trying to get a client out of Afghanistan. I came close to bleeding out on the tarmac. Army surgeons in Kabul fixed me up."

"I'm sorry." Without thinking, she reached out, ran her fingers over the scar on his belly, the heat of contact rushing through her.

His muscles jerked, and he sucked in a breath. "Why are you sorry? You didn't pull the trigger."

She drew her hand away and then wished she hadn't. "I know your job comes with terrible risks. I've just never seen scars like these on a man's body."

He grinned, sat up. "I take it you don't date military men."

At least he no longer seemed angry with her.

She shouldn't care about that, but she did. "I don't date

—full stop. I've been a nun for a year and a half, remember?"

God, did that sound like a plea for sex? Was it a plea for sex?

Maybe.

She couldn't imagine a better way to end a year and a half of chastity than crawling between the sheets with Dylan. Just the thought made her belly flutter and left her hot in all the right places.

Just stop! You're on the job.

Besides, she wasn't into casual sex.

Maybe that should change.

"What about before that? You must have had lots of boyfriends."

Was he asking her about her sexual past?

Gabriela got out of bed, found the brush he'd bought for her, started running it through her hair. "Before that, I was in training at Langley—"

Hands on his hips, he stared at her. "*This* is your first mission?"

She hated to admit that. "My first solo mission, yes."

"Damn, girl. When you jump into the deep end, you jump." He picked up a printed menu. "I hope they've got good room service."

Gabriela ordered *perico*—scrambled eggs with peppers, onions, and tomatoes—along with *arepas*, fruit, and coffee. Dylan ordered coffee and *cachapas*, a kind of corn pancake folded around cheese and shredded pork.

While they waited for the food to arrive, Gabriela took a shower, shaving her legs and underarms with Dylan's razor, something she hadn't done in eighteen months. God, it felt good to be completely clean and silky soft again.

She heard a knock at the door.

"Room service!"

She stayed in the bathroom until room service had gone, washing her panties in the sink and hanging them on a towel rack to dry. She and Dylan had agreed that she shouldn't let the hotel staff see her, given that her face was all over the news. She'd already been seen by the receptionist when they'd arrived last night.

She stepped out of the bathroom, going without panties, to find Dylan wearing his shirt again—*damn it*—and breakfast on the table. "*Dios mío*, that smells good!"

She sat and poured them each a cup of coffee. Then she dug in, the buttery taste of the *perico* making her eyes drift shut.

Bliss.

When she opened her eyes again, she found Dylan watching her, a lopsided grin on his face. "What did you eat at the mission?"

She dabbed her lips. "Mostly rice and beans. Sometimes plantains. It was a very plain diet with little variety. We distributed food to the poor there. We tried to live with the same poverty as those we served. How could I think about food when so many families were going days without eating anything?"

His brows drew together in a frown. "You never thought to sneak out to get some chocolate or pizza or a beer?"

"Sneak out—and risk destroying a cover that took so long to build?" She shook her head, reached for her coffee. "I'm stronger than that. Besides, I had no money, no credit card. *Nada*. I didn't take vows, but I lived exactly like the other Sisters."

"I'm impressed. I don't think I could live like a priest for that long." He laughed, shook his head, as if the idea were absurd. Then he lifted his gaze to hers, regret in his gray eyes. "I'm sorry for being an asshole last night. You were doing your job. I just don't like being tricked, and I overreacted. I know it wasn't intentional."

Oh, yeah. She could get naked with him. "Apology accepted."

Dylan was trapped in a tiny hotel room with a sex goddess.

Gabriela wasn't even trying, and still, everything about her screamed sensuality. The sound of her voice. Her scent. The way she moved. Her sweet face. Those lethal curves. The way she moaned when she tasted something delicious. Those big, brown eyes. Her dark, silky hair.

How had he ever believed she was a nun?

While he sorted through the gear in his backpack, she sat on the bed, legs crossed, watching the news for any updates about their situation and taking notes. And she wasn't wearing panties. He knew this because he'd found her panties drying in the bathroom and had ended up half hard just looking at them.

Tiny, pink bikini panties, for God's sake.

NVGs. Body armor. Helmet. M4 rifle broken down. First aid kit. Spare ACUs, socks, and underwear. A billfold full of cash. Condoms left from their black-market op. A bag of coffee beans. One more pack of smokes. Rain gear. Emergency blanket. Emergency food rations. Water filter. A hundred rounds of 5.56×45mm NATO. A hundred rounds of 9mm. The Glock 19.

He checked it, held it out for Gabriela. "It's loaded—fifteen rounds in the magazine and one in the chamber."

"Thanks." She checked it. "Is there any spare ammo?"

He held up a box of fifty. "There's another fifty in my backpack."

She tucked the Glock under her pillow, then got to her feet and stretched, her T-shirt riding up, exposing her belly.

¡Coño! Damn.

He should go back to thinking of her as Sister María. She might go by Gabriela now, but he could treat her the way he'd treated her before—with respect and distance and no hard-ons. Yeah, he could do that.

There was *no way* he could do that.

Her gaze shifted back to the television. "They're not saying anything new, which tells me they don't know anything specific about you—not yet."

He needed to rein in his hormones, get sex out of his head, so he retreated to familiar terrain. "Have you ever shot to kill?"

"I've had firearms training, but I've never fired at a person before."

"Do you think you can do it? That Glock won't help either of us if you hesitate. You have to be able to react and pull the trigger before the bad guys do."

She seemed to consider his question. "I guess I won't know for certain until I'm in that situation, but I have no moral qualms about killing to save my life—or yours."

Dylan kept his gaze on his gear as he repacked it. "We should have an escape plan in case they catch up with us here."

"I'm all for that." She sat beside him, hands in her lap— close enough for him to smell the sweet floral scent of her hair.

Dylan glanced around the room. "If they catch us in here, we're fucked. I wish we had some kind of cams on the lobby or the elevators, but we don't. Apart from our view of the street, we're blind."

"Cobra might be able to hack the hotel's security camera feed. They could tip us off if the National Police or Sánchez's Guachimanes show up."

That was a damned good idea.

"I'll check in and ask. In the meantime, we've got the elevators and the stairwell not far from the door."

"Neither of those will be useful. The elevators have cams, so they'll know right where we are. They would probably anticipate our trying to escape via the stairway and might lock it down or come up that way."

She was sexy—and smart.

Why did she have to be sexy *and* smart?

But she wasn't done. "Our best bet for a quick escape might be to break into an unoccupied room or a supply closet and wait them out."

"How do we know which rooms are unoccupied?"

"Oh, I don't know—maybe we knock?" Her lips curved in a smile that turned him inside out. "Housekeeping!"

It would be so easy to kiss that smile off her face, to push her back onto the bed, to peel off her clothes and—

He shot to his feet, set the backpack down in the corner. "I'm going to the gym."

"The gym?" She seemed to sense his frustration. "Is something wrong?"

Ah, shit. She's probably reading you like a book, cabrón.

He turned his face away from her. "I need to work off some of this stress."

What he needed to work off was his pent-up sexual energy.

He grabbed his key card and headed toward the door. "I won't be gone long."

She didn't seem afraid to be alone. She almost looked relieved that he was leaving. Or maybe he was imagining that. "Have a good workout."

He stepped into the hallway and drew a deep breath, then rode the elevator down to the third floor. The gym was empty apart from a lone attendant, its weight machines ready for him. Then he noticed the sign on the door.

Running or gym shoes only.

He looked at his feet. He'd run in combat boots plenty of times. He opened the door, walked inside.

The attendant saw him. "Señor, I'm sorry, but you must have the right shoes. Did you not see the sign?"

"My luggage was lost in Paris. Boots are all I have right now."

"I'm so sorry. Maybe the concierge can help you shop for new shoes."

"Right." *Shit.*

He took the elevator back up to the ninth floor, let himself into the room, the TV playing some telenovela.

And there on the bed was Gabriela, eyes closed, naked from the waist down, her shirt and bra pulled up to bare her breasts, one hand between her parted thighs, the other stroking a puckered, brown nipple.

¡Coñoooo!

Dylan's heart hit his sternum, blood rushing to his cock.

She opened her eyes, shrieked, and sat up, jerking the covers over her. "I... I didn't hear you come in."

"Obviously." He was hard as a rock, his cock straining against his trousers. He turned off the television. "Were you fantasizing about me?"

"You?" Her eyes went wide, and her cheeks flushed a delicious shade of red, answering his question. "It's been a year and a half—no sex, not even with myself. This is the *first* time I've truly been alone in months, and you have to walk in—"

"Hey, don't be embarrassed. You don't owe me an explanation." She was feeling exposed, so he revealed something of himself. It seemed only fair. "Want a confession? I went to the gym to sweat *you* out of my system."

"You did?"

"Yeah." He walked over to stand beside her, caught her chin, and lifted her gaze to his. "Want some help? I would love to make you come."

12

The breath rushed from Gabriela's lungs at Dylan's words. She looked into his eyes, heat shivering through her at the intensity of his gaze, the ache between her legs at war with utter mortification. "You ... you want to make me come?"

He grinned, a sexy smile that made her pulse skip, his voice husky and deep. "I've wanted to fuck you since the moment I found out you weren't a nun."

Her belly fluttered. "Really?"

"Shouldn't you already know that?"

"HUMINT training doesn't make a person psychic."

He ignored that, cupped her cheek, his brow furrowing. "I want you, Gabriela, and you want me, too. I saw you staring at my body this morning. I know what lust looks like in a woman's eyes."

Dios mío.

How was she supposed to say no to *this*?

"Wh-what about my job? Your mission?"

"Who's going to tell?" He pulled his T-shirt over his head, tossed it onto the floor. "I sure as hell won't."

She couldn't keep her gaze off him, his muscles shifting as he bent down to remove his boots. "You're getting ahead of yourself, aren't you? I haven't said yes."

"You will."

Oh, he was cocky, so sure of himself, so confident that she wanted him.

And damned if Gabriela didn't find it hot. "I've been celibate for years. I've probably forgotten how to do this."

"It looked to me just now like you remember the basics." He kicked his socks and boots aside.

Her cheeks flamed.

"What do you say we end your celibacy right now?"

And *that* was it.

"Stop talking and kiss me." Gabriela's heart raced, a kind of excitement she hadn't felt for ages washing through her.

"Yes, ma'am." He knelt beside the bed, cupped her face in his hands, his gaze meeting hers for a moment before he brushed her lips with his, once, twice.

She sucked in a quick breath, the contact making her lips tingle.

He leaned in, did it again, made her shiver. "You like that."

"You're teasing me."

"I'm *learning* you." His eyes drifted shut, and he canted his head, taking her mouth with his in a slow kiss.

It was nothing more than lips against lips, but it left her breathless, turned her body to liquid.

Forgetting that her bra and T-shirt were rolled up, she let go of the covers, slid her fingers into his hair, whimpering as he pressed the kiss deeper, teasing her with skilled strokes of his tongue. Then the tips of her nipples brushed the hard wall of his chest, sending a shockwave of pleasure through her, making her gasp.

But he'd felt it, too.

He groaned, broke the kiss, then jerked her T-shirt and bra over her head, leaving her naked. His gaze fixed on her bruised breast. "Did he do this?"

"It doesn't matter now." She pushed the covers aside to reveal all of herself and drew him onto the bed.

Still wearing his ACU trousers, he straddled her hips, his body hard, his size overwhelming her in the best possible way. His gaze moved over her, fixed on her breasts, his brow furrowing. "*Tan hermosa.*"

So beautiful.

Men had said that before, but it hadn't affected her the way it did now.

He palmed her with a callused hand, first one breast, then the other, caressing her, teasing her, making her burn.

She arched into his hands, her eyes drifting shut. Oh, how she had missed this—the heat of a lover's touch. "God, *yes.*"

Then he lowered his mouth to her and sucked one puckered nipple into the wet warmth of his mouth.

She moaned, her body tensing at the exquisite sensation as he licked her, suckled her, plucked her with his lips. He didn't rush, but kept at it, lavishing attention on each breast in turn until she was out of her mind with arousal, her hips rocking beneath him, her body seeking release, endless months of sexual denial flaming inside her.

He chuckled, blew hot breath across her aching nipples, making them draw tighter. Then he stretched out beside her and slid a hand down her ribcage and over her belly to cup her, his gaze soft. "Pick up where you left off. Show me what you like."

Gabriela's heart gave a hard knock. She'd never touched

herself in front of a man before—not counting what had happened earlier.

Dear God, how was she ever going to live that down?

"Don't be shy." He kissed her cheek, the tip of a nipple, then bent one of her legs. "Your knees were up like this and spread wide open."

She didn't know whether to feel embarrassed—or turned on. She closed her eyes, reached down, and ran her fingertip over her swollen clit, slowly at first, then faster.

"I could watch this all day." His fingers joined hers, exploring her, taking over with a deftness that left her aching.

She'd forgotten how good it felt, and it *was* good, *so* good.

He kept up the rhythm then slid a finger deep inside her, making her moan.

"You're so wet." He stroked her, inside and out, his mouth pressing kisses to her cheek, her forehead, her breast.

Pleasure lifted her higher and higher until she was soaring—and then shattered. She cried out, bliss scorching through her, bright and blazing, leaving her breathless, weak, satisfied.

Dylan watched Gabriela as she came, heaven shining on her beautiful face, a strange warmth in his chest. He stayed with her until her peak had passed, kissing her cheeks, her forehead, her hair as she went limp beside him. "Chastity defeated."

Her lips curved in a sleepy smile, her eyes still closed.

Coño, she was beautiful.

Dylan couldn't think of a time when he'd wanted a woman more, lust for her pounding in his chest, as primal as a pulse.

Her eyes fluttered open, her pupils dilated, her gaze soft. "You're good."

"Oh, don't judge me yet, *mi amor*. You haven't put me to the real test."

She slid a hand up his chest. "Are you always so sure of yourself?"

"Always." He settled himself between her thighs, kissed her long and slow and deep, her hands reaching down to unzip his fly.

He knew she thought he was going to fuck her now, but he had other plans.

He let her push his trousers down but stopped her when she tried to take his cock in hand. "Not yet."

He had one shot at this, and he couldn't pull the trigger too soon.

He dragged his mouth from hers, kissed the sensitive skin beneath her ear, let his lips go wherever they chose— her collar bone, the soft curve of her shoulder, the underside of her breasts, a sweet dark nipple.

Her hands explored his shoulders, fingers curling at his nape, her rapid breathing and tight nipples proof that she was aroused again.

He had her right where he wanted her.

He kissed his way down her body, taking his time, savoring the scent and softness of her skin, kissing, licking, nipping until she whimpered.

Without lifting his lips from her skin, he scooted downward, bringing his face between her thighs, her scent drawing him in—musky, feminine, sexual.

Her fingers curled in his hair as if to stop him. "I don't shave there."

As if he hadn't already noticed the V of dark curls.

"I imagine most nuns don't." He chuckled. "Relax. I'm not into twelve-year-olds. I like adult women to look like adult women."

Her pupils dilated, and her grip on his hair loosened, her lips curving into a lethal smile. "You are too much."

"I'm just getting started." He parted her, let his tongue get a feel for her clit, exploring her, making her shiver. Then he got down to work, flicking her clit with his tongue, sucking it into his mouth, tugging on it with his lips. "God, you taste good."

"*Dylan!*" Her response made his cock ache, her every breath a moan, her fingers clenched in his hair, her knees drawn back to her chest to give him plenty of room, any inhibitions she might have had lost in raw sexual need.

He accepted her unspoken invitation, thrust two fingers deep inside her, and was rewarded with a cry. His balls drew tight at the hot, slick feel of her. His cock would be inside her soon, thrusting just like this.

But not yet.

Her eyes were closed, her body trembling, her breath coming in ragged pants, her hands holding his head in place. Then she cried out, her back arching off the bed as orgasm took her again, her muscles clenching around his fingers.

Dylan's heart thrummed in his chest, his need for her driving everything else from his mind, her scent on his skin, her taste on this tongue.

Condoms, cabrón.

He got up from the bed and shucked his trousers, then

fished the unopened box of condoms out of the backpack and stretched out beside her again.

Her eyes were still closed, her body languid and lush and lovely, the sight of her putting that strange pang in his chest again.

What the hell was that?

She opened her eyes and took the condom from him. "On your back, seaman."

"Yes, ma'am." He did as she asked, his cock straining for her, his body tense with unspent sexual need.

She held up the condom. "We don't need this. I've got an IUD. The Agency paid for it before I was sent to Peru in case I was... captured."

Raped.

That's what she meant, but she didn't say it.

He reached up, cupped a breast, savoring the feel of her. "You've been celibate for a while now. I haven't. I won't put you at risk."

She stared at him, surprised. "A guy who *offers* to wear a condom."

"I try not to be a dick."

She set the condom on the bed, straddled his hips, and kissed his sternum. "I love your body."

"It's all yours."

She kissed and licked his nipples, caressed and licked his scars, traced the outline of his muscles, her lips and fingertips spreading fire over his skin. Then she took his cock in hand and stroked him from base to tip and back again.

He stopped her after a few sweet strokes, afraid this would be over before it started. As turned on as he was, he wasn't sure how long he'd last, even with a condom. "I want to be inside you."

Her gaze shot to his. "I bet you say that to all the nuns."

He laughed. "Just you."

She wet him with her tongue—*¡coño!*—then rolled the condom onto his cock.

It was the sexiest fucking thing he'd ever seen—her straddling him, taking his cock inside her tight heat, her eyes drifting shut, a look of pleasure spreading over her face. God, it felt incredible, her body gripping him like a fist.

He reached down to tease her clit with one hand while the other played with a breast, holding himself still below her, letting her set the pace, watching as she ground her clit against his pubic bone. He couldn't get off like this, but that was a *good* thing. It gave him the time he needed to make her come again.

Her palms splayed on his chest for balance, she moved faster, her lips parted, her gaze fixed on his, a look of pleasure-pain in her eyes. "You... feel... *so*... good... inside... me."

Her breathy words sent a jolt of heat to his cock.

She came fast, her head falling back on a moan, her body shaking.

And then he could hold back no more.

He gripped her hips and thrust himself into her, driving hard. He wanted her, wanted all of her. "Gabriela... Fuck!... *Dios mío... Mi amor.*"

Orgasm washed through him, drowning him in pleasure, leaving him to float, his body replete, his mind blown.

BEEP BEEP. *Beep beep. Beep beep.*

Gabriela heard the noise but was too sleepy to care.

Beep beep. Beep beep. Beep beep.

Dylan shifted, drawing away from her, his motions waking her. "*Mierda.*" *Shit.*

She lifted her head, missing the warmth of his body. "What is it?"

He turned off the alarm on his phone and stood, still naked. "Time to check in with the boss."

"Oh. Right." That was important.

She watched as he dialed the number, her gaze moving over him, her body still singing. My God, the things Dylan could do with his tongue...

"Hey, Tower. Cruz here." He paced slowly back and forth while he spoke, the muscles of his bare ass shifting as he moved, that incredible cock of his sexy even when it wasn't hard.

Did he have any idea how good he was in bed?

Yes, he did. Of course, he did.

Oh, don't judge me yet, mi amor. *You haven't put me to the real test.*

He had so much confidence—and control. Then again, he was a former SEAL and had served with DEVGRU. Her boyfriend from college had been a business major.

"Ms. Marquez suggested you hack the security feed from... Oh. Great. Fantastic." Dylan looked over at her, his gaze sliding over her. "Right. Yes, sir."

Gabriela got out of bed, walked to the refrigerator, and pulled out a bottle of water—only to find Dylan staring at her ass when she turned around.

And that gave her a wonderful, terrible idea. If this didn't test his self-control, nothing would.

She took a drink, walked over to him, and knelt on the floor in front of him.

He started to step back, but she took hold of his cock, bringing him to an abrupt halt. "I understand, sir."

She stroked him to hardness with her hand then let her mouth join in the fun, working the length of his erection from base to tip and back again.

He watched her, his pupils wide, his expression strained, the fingers of his free hand sliding into her hair. "No, I wouldn't want that to happen. Her face is on every news station here. Even without the habit, she's easy to recognize."

Gabriela could hear the tension in his voice, but she'd bet his boss couldn't. She worked faster now, her gaze locked with his, her mouth and hand moving together, her tongue teasing the thick head of his cock.

His eyes drifted shut, his fingers clenching in her hair. "No, sir. She's been following the news here. They haven't released a description of me. All they've said is that I'm armed, dangerous, and from the US."

His hips began to move, urging her to go faster.

She did her best to match his rhythm, her tongue keeping up its assault.

"Ms. Marquez? She's... um... been through a hard time, but she's handling it like a professional. She's taking it all... all of it... really well."

Gabriela had to fight not to laugh.

"Yes, sir. I will. Thank you. Talk to you then." Dylan ended the call, threw the phone onto the bed, both hands fisting in her hair. "¡*Carajo*!"

Faster, harder.

His balls drew tight, and she knew he was close.

"*Gabriela*!" He pulled free of her mouth as he came.

She finished him with her fist, cum spurting in white bursts onto her breasts.

He caught her chin, tilted her head back, looked into her

eyes. "You've been a very naughty girl. You could have gotten me fired."

"You did just fine. As you said, I'm handling it like a professional—taking it all."

He grinned, his gaze dropping to her chest. "Come."

He cleaned her up in the bathroom, and they crawled back into bed, Gabriela resting her head on his chest.

"What did he say?"

"They've already hacked the hotel's security feed. I should have known Shields would be on top of that."

"*Elizabeth* Shields?"

"Yeah. You know her?"

"I know *of* her. She fought hard to make the Agency take sexual harassment seriously. There are a lot of women who are grateful to her."

"How about Holly Andris? She used to work for the Agency, too. Do you know her? I think her maiden name was something like Bradshaw."

Gabriela lifted her head, stared at him. "Holly Bradshaw? You work with Holly Bradshaw?"

He nodded. "She and her husband, Nick Andris, both work for Cobra."

That meant Cobra was, indeed, a top-notch company.

"Holly is a legend. Can I meet her?"

"I don't see why not. I'll introduce you next time you make it to Denver."

Gabriela rested her head against his chest again, his heartbeat steady beneath her ear. "What else did your boss say?"

"He wants us to lie low for another twenty-four to forty-eight hours while they work out transportation to San Cristóbal. They're close to a deal with a Colombian guerilla group to smuggle us across the border."

Gabriela played with Dylan's chest hair. "How am I going to pass the time stuck in this room for another day or two with a cocky SEAL?"

"I have no idea. I'm stuck with a spy." He chuckled, flipped her onto her back, and pinned her arms over her head. "We'll have to get creative."

13

D ylan sagged against Gabriela, his cheek resting against her left breast, the bliss of climax leaving him floating. For a time, he lay there, his brain empty, his body satisfied. "I can feel your heartbeat."

It was beginning to slow, just like his.

"Does my boob make a good pillow?"

"The best." But he needed to pull out before the condom slipped off.

He reached down, took hold of the condom and withdrew, tossing the rubber in the trash. Then he wiped off with a tissue, lay beside her, and drew her into his arms.

Outside their window, it was dark.

She rested her head on his chest, tucked one knee between his, her fingers sliding through his chest hair. "So far, being stuck in a hotel room with an arrogant former SEAL hasn't been all that bad."

"Yeah? I think it's gone pretty well, too. I've learned that not all spooks are know-it-all pains in the ass."

She laughed. "How many undercover officers have you met?"

"None."

"That's what I thought."

He wanted to know, so he asked. "Why did you sign on with the Agency?"

"They recruited me out of college. I was just finishing a double degree in criminal justice and international relations when they invited me to apply."

"You could have gone on to do almost anything."

"It's hard when you're five-four and female to get people in law enforcement to take you seriously. But the Agency did."

"How did you end up down here wearing a habit?"

"That's a long story."

"We've got plenty of time."

"I was thirteen when there was an attempted coup against the socialist government. My parents wouldn't let me come to Venezuela that summer, afraid I'd be in danger. In the years after that, I watched life for my family here go from bad to worse. The president was re-elected. Everyone believed he would save us. Then thirty-percent inflation became triple-digit inflation.

"Crime exploded. My Tío Antonio was carjacked. My cousin Maritza saw robbers shoot and kill her neighbor on his front porch. My cousin Yasmira was abducted by a taxi driver who took all her money at gunpoint and then raped her."

"God, I'm sorry. Did anyone catch these bastards?"

"No." She wished. "It got worse after that. When the new president took over, all he cared about was protecting his power. He used the intelligence service to harass and kill anyone perceived to be a threat, turned districts over to organized crime and drug cartels to patrol, and got into the drug trade. The economy crumbled. Food became scarce. And then my Abuelita Isabel got sick with lymphoma."

Dylan didn't like where this was going. "She's the one who made the *pasticho*?"

"Yes." Gabriela sat up, grief on her face, tousled hair hanging just below her shoulders. "We tried to bring her to the US for treatment, but she didn't want to leave Venezuela. We did what we could to help, sending food and money, but as often as not, it was stolen. There was nothing else we could do. There were no drugs for her, not even morphine for pain. Three months later, she was gone."

Gabriela's face crumpled, tears spilling onto her cheeks. "I felt helpless. I loved her so much, and I never got to say goodbye."

Dylan sat up, too, took her hand. "I'm sorry."

Tears spilled down Gabriela's cheeks. "I hate to think of her suffering. She never did an unkind thing to anyone. She deserved better than that."

"Everyone deserves better than that."

Gabriela sniffed. "I tell myself that she is no longer suffering. She's at peace and with God now. But I miss her."

"Of course, you do." Dylan wiped the tears from her cheeks with his thumbs.

He wasn't unfamiliar with the experience of losing a loved one or watching his community struggle. Hurricane George. Hurricane Irma. Hurricane Maria. Floods. The Caribbean drought. Earthquakes. He and his cousins joked that Puerto Rico was the unwilling star of a reality TV series called *Puerto Rico Se Levanta—Puerto Rico Picks Itself Up*— and it was now Season Ten. But he'd never lost a relative like that.

"I wanted to do *something*, so when they came to me with this idea, I was all for it. When you asked why I became a nun, I told you the truth. This was a job that only I, a Latina who speaks fluent Spanish with a venezolano accent, could do."

Dylan understood now. This wasn't just a job for Gabriela. It was about family. "You're incredibly brave."

She shook her head. "It's nothing like the work Agency officers did during the Cold War, sneaking behind the Iron Curtain, playing cat-and-mouse with the Stasi and the KGB, trying to get intel out of China and North Korea."

Dylan didn't know about that, but he did know a thing or two about cartels. "The Andes Cartel doesn't fuck around. If they'd caught you, they wouldn't have hesitated to kill you in any one of a number of terrible ways."

That didn't seem to scare her.

"Most of the time, I did observed and reported what I saw in coded letters that I mailed to my superiors via Peru. I had no hidden cameras, no radios, nothing that would give me away. I *did* put listening devices in Father Alberto's office and his car, but once those were out of my hands, there was no way for anyone to know I wasn't a Sister."

"The Agency must have gotten a lot of actionable intel from that."

Her brow furrowed. "I didn't get what they wanted most —visual proof tying that *malparido* Luis Sánchez to Sergio Ruiz and the Andes Cartel."

"That isn't your fault."

"Yes, it is. I was indoors when the abduction started. I ran outside and stepped in between Pitón—the man you killed—and the journalists. I should have taken cover and just let the abduction happen. I wasn't able to stop it. Instead, Pitón took me, too."

"You took care of the other hostages and made it easier for us to rescue them."

She smiled. "A *lot* easier. I wrote a coded letter to my contact, disguised as a letter to my Reverend Mother, and gave him our location."

Dylan stared at her, stunned. "That intel came from *you*?"

He remembered what Tower had said in the briefing about the ironclad intel regarding drug trafficking at the Mission—and the location of the hostages.

She laughed, the sound like music to Dylan's ears. "It's amazing the kind of respect you get when people believe you're a religious sister. Even from you."

It was the truth.

"Yesterday, I apologized for swearing in front of you, and now I'm fucking you."

"Funny, isn't it?" She slid her hands over his pecs. "Do you prefer it this way?"

"Oh, hell, yeah." Still, he was curious. "What was it like—being a nun?"

GABRIELA WASN'T sure Dylan would understand. "The experience taught me a lot. It made me a better officer."

Dylan narrowed his eyes. "You're serious?"

"Absolutely. You spec ops guys with your high-tech gear have got *nothing* on nuns when it comes to discipline or attention to detail. I promise you that."

He snorted. "Right."

She'd known he would react that way. "Before they sent me to Peru, I spent six weeks in Chicago with Sister Monica for what I called nun boot camp."

"Nun boot camp? What's that—learning the Rosary, memorizing Bible verses, practicing your 'you should feel guilty' look, a lot of kneeling? I have to say I like you on your knees, by the way."

She ignored his teasing. "Nun boot camp means going to bed at seven-thirty every evening, getting up every day at midnight for Matins, then rising for the day at three-thirty in the morning to pray in silence for three hours before attending Mass."

"Three *hours*?" He gaped at her.

"It's called the Great Silence."

"How much could one person have to say to God, anyway?"

"When you pray for the needs of others—the mother with cancer in São Paolo, the teen in Buenos Aires who's addicted to drugs, the man who lost his job in Bogotá— three hours goes by fast. The Sisters answered prayer requests from around the world."

He seemed to consider this. "I guess that would be a big job."

She found herself smiling at memories. "That first night, I fell asleep during the Great Silence only to wake up when Sister Monica gave me a nudge. She said, 'The Mother Superior will be able to tell whether a Sister is praying or sleeping.' I tried hard not to let it happen again."

"Spec ops guys are up at all hours, too, and the jet lag is real."

"But it's not every single day until you die. Nuns don't get vacation."

Dylan frowned. "No, not every day."

"Every day is pretty much the same—seven prayer times a day interspersed with Mass, two work periods, and a social hour where you're allowed to talk."

"A bunch of women *not* talking?" He raised an eyebrow.

"That's hard for me to believe. Didn't you cheat and just whisper?"

"No! That would have been terrible." She tried to imagine how the Sisters would have reacted had she done that. "I had to know the hymns and all the prayers in Latin."

"That's just memorization. We memorize shit, too."

"We ate in silence whatever they put on our plates— usually rice and beans or rice and boiled frozen veggies. I learned never to hope for anything better."

"We get stuck eating shitty rations, too, sometimes for weeks on end."

"But, again, it's not for the rest of your life. No, Mr. SEAL. The nuns have you beat there."

"Okay, I'll give you that one, too."

"Being a Sister means surrendering your ego completely —and that's something no SEAL or spec ops guy has *ever* done."

"Hey, are you saying we're egotistical?" His lips curved in a smile that made his face almost unbearably handsome.

She shrugged, fighting to stay serious. "If the combat boot fits..."

He wrestled her down into the pillows, overpowering her in the most delicious way, then silenced her squeals with a deep, slow kiss.

God, he knew how to kiss.

He stretched out beside her. "Okay, I'll grant you that nuns seem pretty tough. But you forgot something."

"What?"

"No sex—not even getting yourself off."

Of course, he would think of that.

"Believe it or not, I was too tired even to think of it." She had to laugh at his expression of disbelief. "I'm serious."

"I don't think I've ever been that tired."

"Not even during Hell Week?"

"Not even then. I kept thinking how, after I got through it, I could go home to my girl and get laid."

"You have a girl?" She tried to keep her reaction neutral, grateful at least that he hadn't said *wife*.

"I did then. I don't now." There was a hardness to his jaw that told her this was a sore subject for him.

She couldn't help but feel relieved. "I'm sorry."

"Don't worry about it. I'm not into long-term relationships anyway." He pushed whatever he was feeling aside. "How long did it take you to adapt?"

"At first, I thought the seclusion and silence were going to drive me crazy. But by the time I joined the cloister, I'd come to appreciate the stillness. I'd begun to feel the peace that Sister Monica mentioned. I think that's where nuns and religious sisters get their strength. The hardest part by far was when Sister Monica cut my hair."

"She cut your hair?"

Gabriela ran her fingers through her tangled strands. "See how uneven it is? She took a pair of scissors off her desk, had me kneel on the floor, and cut it short just like they would if I were truly joining the novitiate. It's part of giving up your ego and vanity. I had to fight hard not to cry."

He reached over, ran his fingers through it. "You have beautiful hair."

She told Dylan about meeting dear Reverend Mother Beatrice, the Mother Superior at the cloister in Peru. "She treated me like a beloved Sister and gave me a real-world experience of living in a cloister before I left for the Mission of Our Lady of Coromoto. I adore her. I wouldn't want anything to happen to her or the other Sisters because of me."

"She became part of your cover?"

"Yes, she did. I learned so much from her."

"I saw the Sisters at the Mission. They weren't silent."

"Yes, and, after more than six months at the cloister, it was a change. Life seemed much busier and more hectic at the Mission. The Sisters there work hard every day to feed those in need. They fast on Fridays and save that food for the hungry, too. I know it will probably sound strange to you, but I felt like I was a part of something there, that I was doing something that mattered."

"You were. You were trying to help the US take down narco-terrorists."

He didn't understand.

"No, I was feeding people who had nothing to eat, giving shoes to children with bare feet, taking care of sick people who, like my Abuela Isabel, had no medicine. At times, that work made my real job seem unimportant. But then I would remember that Sánchez, the president, and their corrupt regime were the reason so many are hungry."

All at once, it hit Gabriela in a way it hadn't before.

Her time at the Mission was over.

"Hey, what's wrong?"

"I'm glad I was able to help Dianne and Tim, but now I can never go back." Her throat went tight. "I will never get to work as Sister María Catalina again."

He studied her, confusion on his face. "I would think you'd be glad it's over."

"Then you haven't understood a word I've said." She sat up, got out of bed. "I'm going to take a shower. It's past my bedtime."

She walked into the bathroom, shut the door, and leaned her forehead against it, fighting not to cry.

~

A SENSE of guilt gnawed at Dylan. What the hell had upset Gabriela? Most people would be glad to be done with such a restrictive assignment. Shitty food. Long, hard hours. No sex. No personal freedom.

You haven't understood a word I've said.

He didn't understand—not all of it. He got that she wanted to help the people of her parents' homeland. He understood how hard her grandmother's death must have been for her. But he could not fathom how anyone would find the life she'd described as rewarding. Then again...

He had old high school buddies who'd thought he was crazy to join the Navy and become a SEAL. They couldn't understand why he'd been willing to sacrifice so much of his freedom, endure hardship, and put his life at risk. He'd tried to explain, but for them, life was about chasing tail, drinking, and hanging on the beach. They'd gotten on his nerves, and he'd eventually quit hanging with them.

Now he'd just done the same thing to Gabriela.

You fucked up, cabrón.

It didn't matter what he thought. She'd found value in her work at the Mission, and it had been taken from her by Sánchez and his *sicarios.*

You know what it's like to be forced out of a job you love.

Fuck.

Yeah, he did. He sure as hell did.

He had left DEVGRU because he'd been betrayed, not because he'd wanted to leave the Navy. Turning in his resignation and his gear and walking out of his commanding officer's door was one of the hardest things he'd ever done, harder even than losing Valeria. But he'd at least had some agency.

Gabriela had been abducted trying to save others.

The weight of what he said came down on him.

God, he was a *dick*.

He got to his feet, started toward the bathroom still naked, searching for the words to apologize, but then stopped himself. He shouldn't be getting caught up in her.

Yes, she was smart, drop-dead gorgeous, and amazing in bed. What she'd done while he'd been on the phone this afternoon, going down on him like that—she was a wet dream. He couldn't think of the last time he'd had sex with a woman three times in a single day. Usually, it was one and done.

But he wasn't looking for romance or a partner. He was no good at long-term relationships. Their paths had crossed only because of their assignments, and in a few days, their careers would pull them in different directions. She'd go back to Langley, and he'd head home to Colorado for some serious time off.

What the hell is wrong with you?

It didn't matter whether he wanted a relationship with her or not. He'd hurt her, and he needed to apologize.

He'd almost reached the bathroom door when he heard the water turn on. She wouldn't be able to hear him now. He'd have to wait until she finished with her shower.

Mierda.

He straightened up the bed—they had more or less fucked the covers off—put on his boxers, and picked up the condom wrappers. In a few minutes, the room was as organized as he could make it. He sat on the bed, turned on the TV, and surfed for news.

The water turned off, and the hairdryer came on. A short time later, she stepped out of the bathroom, her dark hair silky and shiny, her curves hidden beneath a towel, the sight of her hitting him in the solar plexus.

She glanced around. "You've been busy."

"Hey, Gabriela, I'm sorry." He searched for an excuse but came up with nothing. "You shared some real stuff with me, and I was an asshole."

"Thanks." She dropped the towel, and he saw to his disappointment that she was wearing her panties, which were apparently now dry. "I know it's hard for most people to understand, so don't worry about it."

Ouch.

He didn't like being lumped in with most people. "Actually, I do understand, at least in part. I didn't leave the SEALs because I was ready to go. I left because I no longer trusted the guys on my Team."

Her slender brows drew together in a frown. "I'm sorry to hear that."

"Trust is everything to operators. You need to know that your guys have your back. If they don't... Yeah. Hell. I don't want to talk about this."

"You don't have to tell me anything you don't want to." Bare breasts swaying, she reached for her T-shirt and drew it over her head. "'I'm sorry' was good enough."

She shut off the light on her side of the bed, set the Glock he'd given her on her nightstand, and knelt to pray.

All Dylan could do was stand there, watching, a strange ache in his chest.

14

G abriela awoke to a kiss.

"That's how it works in the movies, too." Propped up on his elbow, Dylan smiled down at her. "Good morning, gorgeous."

"Good morning." She reached up, cupped his stubble-rough jaw. "Sleep well?"

He kissed her forehead. "I dreamed about you."

"What was I doing?"

"This." He kissed her again, soft and slow.

She could refuse him. He'd made a point last night of letting her know that he preferred being single—his way, perhaps, of making sure she knew this meant nothing. Not that she'd expected more from him. There was no way the two of them could be together. A few days from now, maybe even tomorrow, they'd go back to their lives.

She ought to refuse him, but she wanted him.

After almost two years of no sex, she deserved a little crazy pleasure.

She slid her arms around his neck, gave herself over to

his kisses, his lips doing wicked things to hers. Then he rucked up her T-shirt, his mouth moving to her breasts.

It was heaven.

She ran her hands over his biceps, his rock-hard shoulders, the shifting muscles of his back, the hard feel of him arousing her almost as much as the sweet tug of his lips on her nipples, heat building between her thighs until it was a fire. "*Dylan.*"

He reached down, pulled off her panties, and got to work, bringing her quickly to the edge with clever fingers, making her writhe.

The man had figured her out. That much was certain.

Then he stopped, leaving her on the edge.

She moaned and squirmed in protest, making him smile, his gaze soft.

"Patience, *mi amor.*" He reached for a condom, tore the wrapper with his teeth, and rolled it over the delicious length of his cock.

But she couldn't let him call the shots.

"Not so fast, sailor." She put a hand on his sternum and pushed him away, gratified to see the surprise on his face. Then she turned onto her hands and knees, wiggled her bare ass at him, and watched over her shoulder as his eyes went dark. "You said you like me on my knees."

"*¡Coñooo!*" *Fuck!* He slid his palms worshipfully over the curves of her ass, his gaze all over her, a stricken look on his face.

She didn't have time for this. He'd built this fire. Now he needed to extinguish it. "Fuck me!"

He filled her with a single deep thrust, the thick, hard feel of him making her eyes drift shut. "Is that what you want?"

"God, yes."

He found a rhythm, reaching around to stroke her. The skilled action of his fingers. The silky glide of his cock. That sweet, deep stretch. He was driving her out of her mind, the blaze inside her flaring out of control.

Harder. Faster.

He rammed into her with thrusts that made the bed hit the wall and made her cry out, pleasure drawing tight inside her. And then she was there, on that shimmering edge.

She came hard, her hands fisting in the sheets, ecstasy consuming her, white-hot and incandescent. Dylan drove her orgasm home, then shifted the rhythm, pounding into her, both hands grasping her hips.

"*Gabriela.*" He came with a groan, finishing with three deep thrusts.

He caressed her ass, pressed kisses along her spine, then withdrew, the two of them collapsing onto the sheets, smiles on their faces.

Dylan drew her against him. "God, woman, I can't get enough of you."

"Good."

He chuckled. "Are you going to go to confession over me?"

"No. You have to be repentant. I'm anything but."

They ordered breakfast after that, talking about little things—where they'd grown up, their brothers and sisters, their parents. Then Dylan went to take a shower while she tidied up the bed and got dressed.

"Hey, did you use my razor?" he shouted from the bathroom.

"Of course! I have dark hair, and I haven't shaved for almost two years!"

Then his phone rang. It wasn't check-in time. Had Cobra's hack of the security system spotted something?

She ran to the window, looked outside.

No police. No *Guachimanes*.

Just to be safe, she put on her shoes, checked the Glock, stuck her ID in one pocket and the firearm in the rear waistband of her jeans. Then she picked up the backpack and set it on the bed for him where it would be handy.

"*Mierda!*"

It must weigh fifty freaking pounds.

That's why he has all those muscles.

Dylan strode out of the bathroom in his boxers, his face clean-shaven, his hair wet, phone to his ear. But it was the gravity of his expression that caught her eye—and made her adrenaline spike. "Copy that. We're on our way."

He nodded when he saw her and reached for his trousers. "You're ready. Good."

"What is it?"

"The Agency put an asset into play for Cobra." Dylan jerked his T-shirt over his head, reached for his firearm and holster. "A guy in a blue Chevy Aveo is going to stop out front. He's driving us to San Cristóbal. From there, we make our way to Colombia. He believes you're a nun, so I guess you get to be *Hermana María* again."

"Oh. Okay." She hadn't expected that, but it made sense, given the number of people the Agency was trying to protect. "What about the roadblocks?"

He lifted the backpack, slipped it onto his shoulders. "He's got some kind of government clearance that should get us through."

"He must work for the president or el SEBIN." She followed Dylan to the door, looked back at the room, the hours she'd spent with him here suddenly seeming precious.

It's over.

They had a long, dangerous road ahead of them.

DYLAN GLANCED AROUND for a blue car. "Do you know what an Aveo looks like?"

Gabriela pointed with a nod of her head. "He's over there."

The two of them walked side-by-side toward the light blue sedan, Dylan keeping his gaze on the street around them from behind his sunglasses. "I don't know this Sander guy, our driver, so I don't trust him. Be ready for anything."

"If he was sent for us, then your people and mine must have cleared him."

"If they trusted him, wouldn't they have told him your true identity?"

"They trusted you and didn't tell you."

"Okay, you have a point." He bent down to look through the passenger side window and found himself looking at a middle-aged man with gray at his temples and a mustache and goatee. He spoke the words he'd been told to say. "*¡Qué hay, Sander, mi pana! Vamos a tomar una birra.*"

What's up, Sander, my friend. Let's go get a beer.

Sander smiled. "Climb in. I know just the place."

Dylan opened the rear passenger door for Gabriela, reminding himself that he needed to treat her like a nun once more. "There you go, Sister. Buckle up."

"Thank you." She climbed in, put on her seatbelt.

Dylan closed the door behind her and slid into the front passenger seat, shoving his backpack into the space near his feet. "We need to stop somewhere for bottled water and sunglasses for Sister María and maybe a baseball hat or something. She's too recognizable."

Sander looked over his shoulder, his gaze moving over Gabriela in a way that made Dylan's hackles rise. "She doesn't look like a nun to me, but her face... I think you're right."

Dylan lowered his voice, filled it with menace. "If you betray us or do anything to hurt Sister María, I will rip your tongue out through your asshole. Understood?"

Sander looked both surprised and a little afraid. "*Sí, señor.*"

Gabriela took a different approach. "May God bless you for coming to our aid."

His gaze still on Dylan, Sander answered her. "You're welcome, *Hermana.*"

"Let's go."

Sander drove them to a gas station. "You can get what you want here."

Dylan took some cash out of his pocket, handed it to Sander. "I'm not leaving Sister María. You're going to go in, buy her sunglasses, a baseball cap, and get several bottles of water and some food."

"*Sí, Señor.*" Sander took the money, got out of the vehicle, and went inside.

"You scared him half to death."

"I didn't like the way he looked at you."

"That was nothing compared to the way *you* looked at me when you first saw me in these clothes."

"That's different."

"How is it different?" There was a note of humor in her voice now.

"He doesn't get to look at you like that."

Soft laughter. "I see."

"Watch him. You've got the HUMINT training. If you think he's going to betray us, let me know."

"Of course."

Sander returned five minutes later with two plastic bags of junk food and water, a pair of sunglasses, and a black Leones del Caracas baseball cap. He opened the rear driver's side door, handed the hat and the sunglasses to Gabriela, and set the food and water on the seat beside her. "I hope you're a Leones fan, *Hermana*."

"Thank you, Sander." She put on the hat and glasses. "Is that better?"

Dylan looked back over his shoulder. "Definitely."

They drove through the streets of San Antonio, heading toward the main highway.

"The first roadblock is just ahead." Sander flipped on his radio, turned it to a station that played old-time Venezuelan music. "Just relax and try to act like we are having fun. It's going to be okay. You can trust me."

Gabriela began a light-hearted conversation with him, asking him questions about himself—where he'd gone to school, his favorite soccer team, whether he was married, whether he attended church regularly, where he worked.

She seemed to hang on his every word as if she were interested in even the smallest details of his life. It took Dylan a moment to realize that she was interrogating him, getting him to reveal himself.

Yeah, she was good.

Dylan couldn't have done it. He didn't have the patience or the training to make conversation. It was his job to be the hammer, to bring the pain.

Ahead, traffic slowed and then came to a halt, but Sander left his lane and drove down the center of the road straight toward the roadblock, where men in familiar black uniforms checked IDs and searched trunks.

Guachimanes.

"I hope you know what you're doing." Dylan put his right hand near his concealed pistol.

"Don't worry." Sander took out some kind of government ID, slowed down, and held it out the open window.

A *Guachimán* approached the vehicle, saw the ID—and waved them through.

Dylan exhaled, the roadblock behind them now.

"I told you." Sander grinned. "With my SEBIN pass, no one will stop us."

Dylan hoped he was right.

"THEY CANNOT VANISH like mist or turn into birds and fly away!" Luis shouted into Mono's stupid face. He stated what ought to be obvious. "They are either hiding in the city, waiting for us to give up, or they are trying to reach Colombia. How do we find them? We stop every car on every highway and check every person in every vehicle."

"Si, *Jefe*, we *have* been stopping—"

"Knock on every door in San Antonio. Check every hotel between here and the border. Someone must have seen a nun and a gringo in military gear traveling together."

"It's possible, *Jefe*, that they've gotten help—that someone is hiding them or driving them to Colombia."

Luis thought his head would explode. "You're just thinking of this now? I am surrounded by idiots. Of course, someone is helping them! My brother-in-law, the stupid *malparido*, has made many enemies."

Why his sister had married the bastard, Luis couldn't say. He seemed to delight in humiliating Luis. The longer this dragged out, the higher the chance that his brother-in-law would take notice from his presidential palace and drag Luis through the mud.

"Listen, Mono." Luis placed a controlling hand on Mono's shoulder. "I don't care how many people you have to drag out of their cars. I don't care who you have to kill. Find the nun and that bastard commando—and quickly."

"I think you should increase the reward money, *Jefe*. The US government could be paying people, too, and they have a lot to offer."

Luis stared at his *sicario*, heat burning his face at the idea of the United States paying people to betray their country. "Where does the reward stand now?"

"Ten thousand dollars US."

"Make it twenty."

Mono looked unimpressed. "*Sí, Jefe*."

"What? Is that not good enough?"

"How badly do you want to find them? That is how much you offer."

"Make it fifty." Mono started to speak again, but Luis cut him off. "Make it fifty for now—and I will think about it."

"*Sí*." Mono frowned. "What I don't understand is why the nun went with him. Wouldn't she want to get back to the Mission? Why would she flee her own country?"

"He abducted her. Didn't we already discuss that?"

Ten thousand US dollars was a fortune for most Venezuelans these days. And still, no one had given them up. His *Guachimanes* hadn't found them either.

What if they have already crossed into Colombia?

If they had, Luis' chance to redeem himself would be lost. He would be remembered not as the man who took millions from the US, but as the bastard who'd abducted gringos—and had them stolen away from beneath his nose by US special forces. Not that he had proof they were from the US, but what else could they be?

His men had studied photos of the helicopter and tried to trace its origin but had come up with nothing. Photos of the soldier in the street had proved useless, too, his face concealed by goggles, nothing on his uniform to show he was from the US. Without the man as a prisoner, Luis had no victory, nothing to show his brother-in-law.

As for Sister María Catalina, Mono had asked a good question. If Luis was wrong, if the gringo bastard hadn't abducted her, why was she still with him? Had she chosen dick over Jesus? Or was she a prisoner?

Luis decided to talk to the one person who might have answers. He picked up his phone, called Father Alberto at the Mission. "Tell me about Sister María Catalina."

"Have you still not found her?"

"No, but we are close," Luis lied. "What do you know about her?"

"She was quiet, submissive, prayerful. She worked hard and rarely said a word. She came to us from a very strict convent in Peru because she wanted to help her people. The Reverend Mother there was very taken with her and sad to see her leave."

"I know she stayed in touch with the Reverend Mother. Pitón even let her send a letter." Luis went back to his question. "She must have family here."

"I was under the impression they'd all died or left the country."

"Is there any chance she saw something while she was at the Mission? Could she have known what was in those trucks?"

"I don't see how she could have. I keep all the Sisters indoors when the trucks are unloaded. You know that."

Father Alberto was quiet for a moment. "But if she did, perhaps the DEA wants her as a witness."

And it all made sense.

The US government believed she knew something and wanted to use her to get an arrest warrant for Luis.

"You must find her, Luis. Mother Narcisa is quite distraught."

"I should have told Pitón to return her and shot him myself."

"But you didn't, and now you have lost her." Father Alberto's disapproval was clear. "When is the next shipment arriving? We need more food here at the Mission."

Luis needed the money. "I'll call Sergio and tell him we're ready for more."

"He cannot delay. We are feeding hundreds each day."

Luis didn't give a damn about feeding people. "If the nun shows up there—"

"I'll welcome her home—and question her." Father Alberto paused for a moment. "If you find her, do nothing hasty. She is likely an innocent in this."

"Why would I hurt a nun?" Stung by this insult, Luis ended the call.

He thought for a moment about what he wanted to say to Sergio. The bastard was as arrogant as Luis' brother-in-law, but he took Luis seriously.

Then it hit Luis.

If the gringo was on his way toward Colombia, perhaps it was time to bring Sergio and his Andes Cartel into the search. They controlled that border. Against them, not even the United States had a chance.

15

I t was an eleven-hour drive from San Antonio de Los Altos to San Cristóbal, but between roadblocks, toll booths, and bathroom breaks, it seemed to drag on forever, boredom interspersed with bursts of adrenaline. Every time they had to stop for Sander to show his SEBIN pass, Gabriela's pulse picked up.

But so far, so good.

Sander, it turned out, had led an interesting life, working as an accountant for Petróleos de Venezuela, S.A., the state-owned petroleum company, before the industry fell into ruin. After that, he'd taken a job with SEBIN, managing their payroll, a position that enabled him to see and hear much and which made him an ideal Agency asset.

"If they find the two of you, I know what they'll do." He shared this as if Gabriela and Dylan had no idea they'd be interrogated and tortured. "There's an area in the basement where they take prisoners for interrogation. People go in, but they don't come out. That place is impenetrable. No one has ever escaped. They use torture and sensory deprivation to break—"

"Why do you say things like that in front of Sister María? Are you trying to scare her, man? It's your job to make sure we *don't* get captured."

"*Sí.* Sorry, Sister."

"God will see us through." And if God chose not to get involved, Gabriela had Dylan—and her Glock.

They were on the outskirts of San Cristóbal when she noticed a change in Sander. He was speaking faster now and laughing more, his laughter louder and almost manic, sweat trickling down his temples despite the AC.

He was nervous, panicking about something.

From the top of a hill, Gabriela saw through the windshield into the valley below. Not far ahead was another roadblock, traffic backed up for a quarter-mile.

She slipped out of her seatbelt, drew the Glock from the waistband of her jeans, and pressed it to the side of Sander's throat. "Pull off the highway. Now!"

Dylan's gaze jerked to hers, then he drew his pistol, too. "Do it!"

Sander tried to laugh it off, drove faster. "Why are you doing this? I'm your friend. Didn't I get you out of San Antonio? The Agency paid me to—"

"You're about to betray us."

Dylan's gaze was fixed on Sander. "Did you not hear the good Sister, *amigo*? Pull over. *Now!*"

His shout made Sander jump.

Sander flipped on the turn signal and pulled to the side of the highway. "You two are crazy. Haven't I proved myself to you? I brought you safely all this way, and now you point guns at me?"

Gabriela could hear the guilt in his voice. "You're a liar, Sander."

"Everything I've told you is true."

"It's what you haven't told us that bothers me. You plan to turn us over to el SEBIN." Gabriela lowered her pistol, let Dylan handle that part of it. "Why didn't you betray us to your friends at the first roadblock?"

Sander exhaled, squirmed, and broke. "I wanted to get paid by the Agency first. I told them I would bring you to them in San Cristóbal."

"You double-crossing bastard." Dylan looked angry enough to kill.

"Greed is a *mortal* sin, Sander." Gabriela sat forward, spoke next to his ear. "Now you won't get anything—no more money from the Agency and nothing from Sánchez or the Andes Cartel, either. They're going to think you betrayed them. Worse than that, you've exposed yourself as a CIA asset. You know what el SEBIN does to traitors."

Dylan held his pistol steady. "Should I blow his brains out here?"

"No." Gabriela glanced over her shoulder, checking traffic. There couldn't be witnesses. "Give me your phone, Sander."

"Slowly," Dylan cautioned him. "I won't hesitate to pull the trigger."

Sander handed over his phone.

Gabriela pocketed it. "We wait for a break in the traffic, and then search him and put him in the trunk. I'll drive. We'll take side roads into town."

"They'll find you anyway. You can't make it across the border."

Dylan pressed the pistol into Sander's temple. "Open your mouth again, and I'll shut it permanently."

When the road was clear, Gabriela and Dylan stepped out, walked around to the driver's side, and opened Sander's door. "Pop the trunk. Get out. Leave the keys."

He did what they'd told him to do and stepped out of the car, hands raised.

While Dylan held the pistol on him, Gabriela searched first the trunk and then Sander, removing a tire iron from the trunk and a pocket knife from Sander's trousers, along with his pass and his cash. When she was certain he had nothing on him, she gave him a shove. "Climb in. Make it fast."

He hesitated, rage and fear on his face.

"Do what Sister María tells you to do, or I'll kill you here."

Sander climbed into the trunk, glared up at Gabriela. "You're no nun."

"I'm not?" Gabriela feigned shock. "*¡Mierda!*" *Shit.*

"I'll tell them." Sander laughed, a sick, terrified sound. "They still think you're a nun, but when they find out—"

"Watch what you say, *hijoeputa.* Those words will get you killed." Dylan slammed the trunk.

Gabriela hurried to the driver's seat. "We need to turn around and head back to the last exit. We can use your phone to navigate."

When he got back into the passenger seat, Dylan had a big grin on his face. "I like watching you work."

"THERE'S A BRIDGE UP AHEAD." Dylan glanced up from his phone, his M4 back in one piece and in his lap. Because they were escaping rather than evading, he'd put on his gear again—camo shirt, body armor, chest rig, helmet with NVGs. "I hope it's wide enough for the vehicle."

He'd hate to have to retrace their route and try again.

In the valley below, the lights of San Cristóbal glittered, seeming as distant as they'd been an hour ago.

Sander's phone buzzed again with another message from an unidentified number.

```
Where the fuck are you, you bastard!
```

Dylan typed in a response.

```
We stopped outside Santa Barbara. The nun
has to pee again, you stupid cocksucker.
```

He chuckled as the next message arrived—nothing but profanity.

"I don't like this." Gabriela glanced over at him, worry on her face. "How do we know the guerillas won't betray us like Sander did? They have close ties to the cartels and no love of the US. An Agency officer and a Navy SEAL are a valuable prize. They could take us prisoner and try to sell us back or kill us and turn our bodies over to Sánchez to exhibit on the news."

Dylan didn't like it either. "We ought to find a way into Colombia ourselves."

She shook her head. "That would be hard. The guerillas and cartels control all of this—the border, the jungle, the river. They use these mountain roads to smuggle. They know where the Rio Táchira is safe to cross, and they watch those areas."

"Then we cross where it's not safe. Can you swim?"

She nodded. "In a swimming pool, yes, but I'm not a SEAL. In some places, the banks are steeper, and the river is faster and much deeper."

He reached over, rested a hand on her shoulder. "I can

get you across, Gabriela. I've made my way through territory much more hostile than this and come ashore through pounding surf far more dangerous than anything the river can throw at us."

A small wooden bridge loomed ahead of them.

"That's the bridge?"

"Stop here. Let me check it out."

The moment the vehicle stopped, Sander began screaming and shouting, perhaps believing that there were others around, someone who might hear.

Rifle in hand, Dylan got out of the Aveo, lowered his night-vision goggles into place, the landscape around him taking on a green glow.

No movement, no sign of human beings.

He walked to the bridge, looked down to find a rocky ravine perhaps twenty feet deep. He walked across, tested the bridge's strength. The wooden beams creaked, but they seemed free of rot and sturdy. But would they hold the weight of a car?

There was only one way to find out.

He motioned Gabriela forward, gestured for her to steer a little to her left, gave her a thumbs-up. Wood groaned as the front tires moved onto the bridge, riding on the very edge of the structure. Dylan walked backward, signaling her to keep moving forward, his gaze on the front tires.

If she moved even an inch to one side or another...

Slow and steady.

His feet hit dirt, and a moment later, the car's front tires did the same. He stepped aside, making room for the vehicle to pass.

Gabriela stopped, spoke in a silky voice. "Hey, stranger. Need a lift?"

Dylan climbed in, lifted the goggles. "Teamwork."

Then he noticed the digital display. *¡Coño!* "Let's pull into that clump of trees and turn off the lights. I'm late checking in with Tower."

Tower answered on the first ring. "You're late. What's your situation?"

"The Agency asset betrayed us, but Ms. Marquez was onto him and saved our asses." Dylan quickly explained. "The bastard is locked in the trunk."

"He's a liability. You might have to dispose of him."

"I know." Dylan wasn't sure what Gabriela would think about killing an unarmed prisoner. He didn't like it himself, but he couldn't let Sander give them away.

"Sánchez's men are probably searching for that vehicle."

"We're hoping to ditch it once we get into San Cristóbal." He decided to come right out with it. "After what happened today, neither of us wants to risk putting our lives in the hands of guerillas or smugglers. They're too closely tied to the Venezuelan government and the cartels. I'd rather figure it out from here on our own."

"The Agency isn't going to like that. They've cut some arms deal with the guerillas—a certain amount of military hardware in exchange—"

"Fuck the Agency!" Dylan didn't want any part of that. "If we'd followed their last plan, we'd be in Sánchez's hands by now."

"The Agency authorized this operation. They're paying for it. I can't tell them to fuck themselves."

Dylan opened his mouth to speak, but Tower cut him off.

"But I *can* tell them that their asset betrayed you and that you had to go to ground. I'll tell them I don't know where you are."

"Good enough."

"Listen to me, Cruz. No matter what, do *not* let yourself be taken or killed. The political fallout would be disastrous."

No pressure. "Understood."

"I'm trusting you to get yourself and Ms. Marquez out of there alive."

"I'll get the job done."

"I know you will. And Cruz?"

"Yes, sir?"

"Godspeed."

"Thank you, sir." Dylan ended the call, found Gabriela watching him. "He cut us loose. We're on our own."

"I NEED TO ELIMINATE SANDER." Dylan said this out of the blue.

Gabriela's stomach knotted. "Couldn't we just gag him and tie him to a tree?"

They had to do something. She understood that. They couldn't allow him to give them away—or to reveal to SEBIN that they'd been here.

Dylan took a suppressor out of his backpack, screwed it onto the barrel of his pistol. "We can't take him with us, and if we leave him behind, he'll eventually tell his bosses everything he knows, including the fact that you're an Agency officer."

It was true—every word.

"I'll make it quick and painless, which is more than el SEBIN will do. You don't have to see it or be a part of it."

"I'm not weak."

"I know you're not, but you're not used to this."

"Are we sure there's not another way?"

Dylan shook his head. "He made this choice for us when he decided to betray us."

It hadn't upset Gabriela when Dylan had killed Pitón. In fact, she'd told him to pull the trigger. The bastard would have killed her. What Dylan was doing now made operational sense. But Sander was unarmed and a prisoner.

He was ready to hand you and Dylan over to Sánchez.

"Pop the trunk." Dylan climbed out, taking his rifle with him.

Gabriela pulled the lever, watching in the rearview mirror as Sander climbed out, rumpled and angry.

"Were you going to leave me in there all night, you stupid bastard?"

"Do you want to piss or not?" Dylan gave Sander a shove. "Into the trees."

Sander walked ahead of Dylan into the forest.

Gabriela squeezed her eyes shut but heard nothing.

A few minutes later, Dylan reappeared, pistol pointed at the ground.

He climbed into the car. "He didn't see it coming."

Gabriela nodded and swallowed—hard.

"I don't like to kill."

She fought to keep her voice steady. "Of course, you don't."

They drove on, the silence interrupted by Dylan's directions.

"A right here should take us into the city."

A *chigüire*—or capybara—ran in front of the car. Gabriela gasped and slammed on the brakes. The animal scurried across the road and into the trees.

Dylan rested a hand over hers. "It's okay."

She met his gaze, doing her best to put her emotions aside. There was no room for compassion in a survival scenario. "Thank you for doing what had to be done. You're risking everything to rescue me."

"I'll get you home, Gabriela."

They passed San Cristóbal at nine in the evening, taking back roads toward San Antonio del Táchira, which sat right next to the Rio Táchira and the border.

"Park in that stand of trees." Dylan studied the satellite image on his phone. "We'll set out on foot from here, head north for a while before crossing."

"We should search the car, see if there's anything we can use." Gabriela looked through the glove box and trunk, found a flashlight but nothing else that might be useful. "What about Sander's phone. We shouldn't take it with us."

"I left it with his body so they can find him."

They set out, Dylan with rifle raised, pack on his back. The night was dark, but Dylan used his NVGs to guide them —and watch for the presence of guerillas lurking among the trees. Compared to her, he moved almost soundlessly, each step deliberate, controlled. Then again, he could see much better than she could.

She tripped on a tree root.

A strong arm shot out to steady her. "*Careful.*"

They'd gone for about ten minutes when he motioned for her to get down.

She dropped to the ground, taking cover beside him, Glock in her hand, heart thrumming. She'd begun to wonder if Dylan was seeing things when she heard it— men's voices. Distant at first, they grew nearer.

Then six armed men in black appeared among the trees, headlamps lighting what Gabriela saw was a footpath.

Guachimanes.

Sánchez's men were patrolling the forest, watching the river, searching for them.

"She's a nun, so maybe God is watching over her. Did you think of that?"

"You're a fucking idiot."

"They're probably hiding somewhere in the city, waiting for morning."

"Quiet! Do you want them to hear you coming?"

"What does the boss need us for anyway? He's got drones. They can see in the dark. They'll find them."

"Stop talking!"

Drones equipped with thermal vision?

Shit.

Gabriela's pulse spiked. For the first time since this began, she was truly afraid.

Then from overhead, she heard it—a soft whirring sound.

16

D ylan had only a moment to react. "Stay down. Get ready to run."

He raised the rifle, sighted on the drone, and fired, alerting the *Guachimanes* to their position. Then he switched his rifle to a three-round burst, sighted again.

Rat-at-at! Rat-at-at! Rat-at-at!

Four men fell. The other two ran for cover.

Rat-at-at! Rat-at-at!

"They know we're here." He stood, drew Gabriela to her feet. His last glance at his phone had showed the riverbank no more than a thousand meters west of their position. "We head due west to the river and cross it here."

They moved as quickly as they safely could through the trees, Dylan picking their path and doing his best to guide her. The last damned thing they needed was for her to break or sprain an ankle. That had happened to a human-rights lawyer his Cobra buddy Connor was trying to get out of Myanmar, and it had nearly gotten them both killed.

The terrain became steeper, and the trees began to thin,

making their cover scant. And then it was there, maybe fifty meters downhill below them—the river.

Dylan dropped to his knees, searched the forest around them and the riverbank beyond for any sign of hostiles. "The moment we leave these trees, we'll be visible to any eyes in the sky, as well as anyone watching the water. The river is narrower here, which means it might be faster and a little deeper. We get across as fast as we can, climb up the other side, and shelter among the trees."

Gabriela nodded, catching her breath. "I understand."

He raised his goggles so that he could see her with his eyes. "Prepare your mind for the water to be cold. Don't let that stop you. I'll do my best to stay close, but if you get swept away, aim your feet downstream and use them to keep yourself from hitting submerged rocks. Navigate with your arms to reach the riverbank."

"Feet downstream. Use my arms to steer."

"That's it." He glanced around again. "Ready?"

Gabriela pressed a soft kiss to his lips. "Stay safe. I don't want anything to happen to you. I care about you, Dylan."

His heart seemed to skip a beat, warmth building in his chest. "You take care of yourself. If anything goes wrong, maintain your cover. You're an innocent. I abducted you because I'm a mean, awful gringo."

"I won't say anything to get you killed. Listen to me! You're Cuban, not a gringo. You took me because I saw your face. You promised to let me go when we reached Colombia."

He caught her chin. "Don't worry about me. You do what you have to do to survive and get home."

They stumbled, slipped, and slid their way down the steep embankment, soil shifting beneath their feet.

Dylan clipped his M4 to his chest rig, took Gabriela's

hand, and stepped into the water. It was icy cold and moving fast.

Gabriela sucked in a breath as the water came over her waist. She was shorter than he was and weighed much less than he did, making this harder for her.

"Grab onto the strap of my backpack, and don't let go!"

She reached to do as he'd asked—and the water took her.

Dylan lunged, grabbed for her, but she vanished beneath the surface, her baseball cap floating free and disappearing downstream.

Gabriela!

He watched for her, saw her surface a few meters away, her feet pointed downstream, her arms paddling desperately.

He let the current take him, too, but he had much more experience in the water. Using his arms to propel himself toward her, he managed to get in front of her.

She crashed into him, coughed, her arms wrapping around his neck.

"I've got you." He kicked hard and paddled with one arm, bringing them both to the other side. "Are you okay?"

She nodded, shivering. "J-just c-cold."

There wasn't anything he could do about that now. They were visible to anyone with eyes on the river—and that included fucking drones. They'd lost time, and they'd gone a good two hundred meters downstream from their original position.

"We need to move." He drained the water out of his M4, looked up the bank, unable to see over it to what might lie beyond. "Do you still have the Glock?"

She nodded, drew it from her waistband, shook out the

water, then slipped it back into her jeans, and covered it with her T-shirt.

"Let's go."

The two of them scrambled up the riverbank.

He reached the top first and knelt, searching the forest with his NVGs for any sign of people, but the landscape was hilly, making it impossible for him to see what lay beyond the rise. He was certain the bad guys were on their way. The drone had gotten a good look at them before he'd shot it down. It would have sent their GPS position.

Gabriela crawled up beside him, her wet clothes muddy, mud caking her shoes and her hands, a streak of mud on her cheek. "Is the coast clear?"

"For now."

The land sloped upward, trees growing thicker around them, offering them cover from people, but not from drones.

They reached the top of the rise—and froze.

¡Puñeta! Fuck!

Below them were at least twenty men, all armed, rifles pointed at them.

Dylan dropped his M4, raised his hands, rage burning white-hot through him.

A tall, overweight man in a Hawaiian shirt stepped forward, a grin on his fleshy face. "Welcome to Colombia."

At the sight of Sergio de Anda Ruiz, Gabriela's heart hit her breastbone—a thud of terror. She let her training carry her, slipping into the personality of Sister María once again, allowing her fear and her shivering to work for her. "*¿Son policías? ¿Son católicos?*" *Are you police? Are you Catholic?*

Snickers.

Ruiz smiled. "Sí, *Hermana*."

She sank to her knees, crossed herself, and began to pray, her body still shivering from her swim in the river. "Mary, Mother of God, I thank you for my deliverance."

She went on, words of thanksgiving spilling from her lips in a rush, until Ruiz walked up to her.

He tucked a finger beneath her chin, lifted her gaze to meet his. "You are safe with us, *Hermana* María. We have been searching for you."

"I knew help would come." She took his hand, kissed it. "*Gracias, Señor*."

He tilted his head, frowned at her black eye. "Did he do this to you?"

But Gabriela couldn't cause Dylan any more suffering. "N-no, *Señor*. Pitón did when I r-refused to lie with him. That one k-killed him."

Ruiz lifted her to her feet. "We have many questions for you, *Hermana*. We're taking you home. Bring him."

Men rushed in on Dylan, struck him, drove him to his knees, each blow making Gabriela's heart constrict.

Ruiz led Gabriela downhill toward a clearing where there were more men and several vehicles. He shouted to his men. "Don't kill him! He needs to be alive for the reporters. Our partner in Venezuela will decide what to do with him."

Reporters?

Shit!

They would parade Dylan in front of the cameras—the very thing the US had wanted to avoid at all costs—and then they would torture and kill him.

"I-I need to let Mother Narcisa kn-know that I'm safe—and Father Alberto."

"We will let them know. You are soaking wet and shivering."

"I t-tried to get away from h-him on the w-water, but he was f-faster and stronger."

"Of course, he was. He is a military man, and you are a young woman and small." He called to one of his men. "Get me a blanket for the good Sister."

Good Sister.

Ruiz didn't fool her. They planned to interrogate her, too, to find out as much about Dylan as they could and to understand why he'd taken her. They wouldn't hesitate to kill her if they believed she knew something about their smuggling operation at the Mission. If they discovered she wasn't a nun, they'd take turns raping her first.

Ruiz led her to a Land Rover, where one of his men opened the rear passenger side door and helped her inside. Ruiz took a wool blanket from one of his men and handed it to her. "This should warm you, *Hermana*."

"Bless you for your kindness, *señor*."

He stood there for a moment, watching her. "Do you not know who I am?"

Gabriela looked him straight in the eyes, enjoying this moment. "I'm sorry, *señor*, I do not. I have lived much of my life cloistered and am not a worldly person."

She could tell that this came as a blow to his ego, but he brushed it aside. "Of course, *Hermana*. I am Sergio de Anda Ruiz, a well-known Colombian businessman. These men you see—they are my army."

"I am grateful to you, Señor Ruiz, and to your army." She let tears come into her eyes. "You have rescued me against all hope."

He got into the front passenger seat, shouted for his driver, another man getting into the back seat with Gabriela, rifle in hand.

Gabriela caught just a glimpse of Dylan being dragged

to a white van and shoved into the back but did her best to show no emotion, comforted only by the Glock jabbing her in the back. In the dark, no one had noticed her weapon, and, so far, they hadn't searched her.

"Don't worry about him. We will take care of him."

Gabriela gave Ruiz a grateful smile. "I just want to be back at the Mission and wearing my habit and veil once more."

"He forced you to dress like this?"

"He stole these clothes and made me wear them. He said I was too recognizable."

"*Malparido gonorrea.*" *Gonorrhea bastard.* "Pardon me, Sister."

"You have done a good thing today, Señor Ruiz. I'm sure that God forgives you."

Gabriela held the blanket close, closed her eyes, did her best to listen.

"We take them back to San Antonio del Táchira and wait. Our associate is inbound on a helicopter and is bringing media with him. Then we hand them over."

Somehow, Gabriela had to free Dylan and escape Ruiz and his men before this associate—almost certainly Luis Sánchez—arrived with the reporters.

If she failed, everything they'd suffered and struggled for would be for nothing—and Dylan would die.

HANDS TIGHTLY BOUND, Dylan sat with his back in the rear corner of the van, ignoring the taunts from Ruiz's men and the pain in his right side, his mind on his breathing—and his botched mission.

He wasn't used to failure. It had never been an option,

and it wasn't an option now. But if he didn't escape with Gabriela soon, he would have blown everything. He would fail Cobra. He would fail Gabriela. He would fail his country.

Unless he found a way out of this, his face would be all over the news soon, creating a crisis for Cobra, which might go bankrupt from lack of Pentagon business, and for the US government, which would deny knowing anything about him.

"We're supposed to take them back across to San Antonio and wait. Sánchez is coming in one of his helicopters and bringing reporters. After the press conference, who knows what they'll do to him."

"Watch what you say in front of the prisoner, *malparido*."

"He's a gringo. He probably doesn't understand Spanish. Besides, what can he do? He's beaten, outnumbered, helpless as a little girl."

Dylan said nothing, but the bastard wasn't wrong. He'd taken a kick to the side where his body armor didn't protect him, leaving him with bruised ribs that made it painful to breathe. There were at least twenty armed hostiles—five in the back of the van alone. And he and Gabriela were separated. He'd seen her get into a Land Rover with that bastard Ruiz.

Despite the gravity of the situation, he almost smiled. She was amazing, harnessing her very real fear of Ruiz and the cartel and transforming into fear of Dylan and the desperate relief of a freed prisoner. The bastards had bought it—for now.

Still, they would interrogate her. If they believed she knew about the drug-smuggling at the mission, they would kill her. If they discovered she was a US citizen, not a Venezuelan, they would kill her. If they learned she was an

Agency officer, they would rape her, torture her, and then kill her in some barbaric way.

Torturously cruel killing was the Andes Cartel's specialty.

That's what they're going to do to you—after they parade you around in front of the cameras.

What he needed was a miracle.

Except that he didn't believe in miracles. What most people called miracles were either the result of hard work or freakish good luck. Right now, there wasn't anything he could do, and he seemed to be fresh out of luck.

From outside, came a flash of light followed by a clap of thunder, rain spattering the van's roof. Or was that hail?

Another flash of lightning.

Crack.

The van turned, the road beneath the tires no longer rough dirt but smooth asphalt. They must be getting close to the Venezuelan border.

Flash. *Crack.*

"¡*Coño*!" One stared upward. "*Está cayendo un palo de agua.*"

It's a downpour.

Had they said Sánchez was arriving in a helicopter?

The storm would slow him, too. There was no way a pilot could fly in this. That would at least buy them some time—provided the storm lasted more than a few minutes. The moment it let up, Sánchez would be airborne again.

"Did you see the nun?" said an ugly bastard with acne scars. "Fuck! A chick like that should never be allowed to be a nun. You know what I'm saying? Those tits and that pussy are going to waste."

The men laughed, one making wanking gestures with his hand.

"I bet he fucked her." One of the men kicked at Dylan, struck his boot. "Did you fuck her, asshole?"

"You shouldn't talk that way about a Sister," Acne Man joked. "You'll go to hell for that."

"Just for that?"

More laughter.

Flash. *Crack.*

Acne Man spoke again. "If Don Sergio thinks she's lying or that she knows something, we might all get a chance to stick our dicks in her."

Hijoeputas. Fuckers.

Dylan kept his face impassive as if he had no idea what they were saying, but he'd be dead before that happened.

And what are you going to do to stop them?

Goddamn it!

He wasn't used to feeling powerless or facing a no-win situation.

They must be back in San Antonio del Táchira now. A left. Another left. A right. Then the van went up a hill, made a sharp left—and stopped.

"Everyone out. We're going to wait for Sánchez here. Make sure this bastard doesn't get away. Don Sergio will blow your brains out if you do."

The side door of the van opened, and the men piled out, dragging Dylan with them into the pouring rain.

Five muddy vehicles. The Land Rover.

There was Gabriela, still with Ruiz, disappearing into a grand hacienda.

"Move!" one of the men shouted in English, giving Dylan a shove.

They followed their boss indoors, Dylan's gaze meeting Gabriela's for just a moment, the trust he saw there giving him strength.

"Take him to the basement." Ruiz shut Gabriela in what looked like an office, then walked over to his men. "Interrogate him, but remember, he must be able to speak. He must be able to confess on camera. Do not kill him or leave him unconscious or incapacitated. Our partner wants his prize whole."

Down the stairs they went, rage holding the worst of Dylan's fear at bay. He wasn't a fan of pain, but he wasn't going to let these assholes break him.

Gabriela's life depended on it.

17

Gabriella sat in what looked like an office, still wrapped in her blanket, trying to focus on her interrogation and not what they were doing to Dylan downstairs. She needed to keep her mind clear and her emotions in check. She was sitting across from one of the most dangerous and most wanted criminals in the world.

She couldn't afford to slip up. "He came upon us in the street. Pitón put a gun to my head. But that one shot him and then forced me to hide with him in the basement of an apartment building."

Ruiz watched her, a predator trying to decide whether she was his pet—or his prey. "What is his name?"

"He never told me. He said it was better for me not to know. He wished me to remain silent, which isn't hard for me. He spoke only Spanish to me, Spanish with what sounded like a Cuban accent."

"Did he force you to abandon your vow of chastity?"

"No, señor, he didn't touch me. He didn't try to lie beside me. But even if he had, the sin would be his alone. If a religious sister is raped—God forbid—the sin lies only with the rapist. Because it was not her choice, her vow is intact, and she is still chaste."

Ruiz clearly found that answer boring. "Why didn't he let you go after he killed Pitón? Why did he keep you with him? You're Venezuelan. He must want something from you."

Gabriela channeled all of the tension inside her into her answer, allowing her eyes to fill with tears. "He told me that he couldn't let me go because I'd seen his face. He said he needed a hostage in case he was caught, but he promised to let me go when we reached Colombia. I was afraid he would kill me after we crossed the river, but then you were there."

Ruiz seemed to consider this. "Did you like your life at the Mission?"

She gave him a sad smile. "Oh, yes, Señor. Mother Narcisa is a godly woman. With God's help, we fed many hundreds of hungry people. Father Alberto worked hard to get the food we needed. I was doing God's will there."

"Do you know where that food came from?" Ruiz was trying to find out what she knew about the shipments.

"No, señor, but God provides."

"*I* provide, Hermana. That food came from *me*, my gift to my Venezuelan neighbors."

Did he realize what he'd just admitted? She had it now. She had the proof she needed—straight from Ruiz's bragging mouth.

"From *you*, señor?" She stared at him, feigning amazement. "Thank you for your kindness and generosity. Truly, God will bless you."

"Did you help to unload those shipments?" He wanted to know whether she'd seen the drugs.

"No, Señor Ruiz. I am the newest sister at the Mission and not very strong, so I spent most of my time cleaning or in the kitchen cooking. In the afternoons, I distributed food to the poor if my other work—"

A knock came at the door, interrupting her.

"Come!"

A man with bad acne scars entered, blood spattered on his T-shirt—most likely Dylan's blood. "When is our partner arriving?"

"He is stuck at the airport in Valencia waiting for this storm to end. Has the bastard said anything?"

"Not a word. I've tried electroshock. I can make him scream, but he won't even tell me his name or say where he's from."

Gabriela's heart constricted again, a sharp pang behind her breastbone. She hadn't heard any screams. Which must mean the basement was soundproofed. That made sense if you were a cartel boss. Why have a lovely house if you had to listen to your victims scream while you're eating dinner?

Ruiz frowned. "You'd best stop for now. If he dies, it will be your head. Be careful what you say around him. Sister María tells me he speaks Spanish."

"*Sí, Patrón.*" Rather than looking afraid, the man grinned and was gone, closing the door behind him.

Ruiz studied her. "You don't approve. After all this man did to you?"

"All of this violence—kidnapping, killing, torture. Forgive me, but I have never seen such things before."

"The world is a rough place, Sister María. You are either the wolf or the sheep. Which are you?"

She lifted her chin, drew herself up to her full height. "I am a child of God, as are we all, each of us made in God's image."

He chuckled, got to his feet. "When did you last eat?"

She tried to remember. "This morning, I think."

"I'll have the kitchen prepare you some food while we wait."

She followed him, holding tightly to the blanket, certain they would see the bulge in her T-shirt and discover the Glock now that they were in a lighted house. She did her best to memorize the layout of the place and gauge Ruiz's strength. She thought she'd seen five men take Dylan downstairs. Another two stood just inside the front door, while the majority—about fifteen men—milled about on the covered veranda.

She fought back a wave of despair. She was outnumbered roughly twenty-three to one, and all she had was fifteen rounds in a Glock.

You'll take weapons from the men, use their bullets against them.

She had never been in a gunfight before. She'd only ever fired weapons at paper targets on a range. She'd never killed anyone.

You'll do it—for Dylan.

Ruiz introduced her to a tight-lipped, unhappy-looking cook named Imelda and asked her to make Gabriela a meal. "She's had a rough time, so we must care for her."

Gabriela knew he hadn't made up his mind about her yet.

"Thank you, Señor. God bless you for your kindness." *You bastard son of a bitch.* "I am grateful."

She had to find a way out of this—and soon.

DYLAN PRETENDED TO BE UNCONSCIOUS, hoping to seem weaker than he was and to buy himself some time to recover, his skin shrinking from that last shock. The bastards had stripped him down to his trousers and taken turns pounding on him until Acne Man had pulled some kind of homemade electroshock device out of a closet, plugged it in, and showed Dylan what real torture was.

Dylan had been through advanced SERE training—Survival, Evasion, Resistance, and Escape. He'd been interrogated, beaten, threatened with rape, starved, deprived of light and sleep, and submerged in cold water until he'd almost drowned. But he'd known it wasn't real and that it would end.

This wouldn't stop until he was dead—or found a way to escape.

The pain was like nothing he'd been through before, worse even than being shot in the gut. Each time, he'd tried to wrap his thoughts around Gabriela to give him strength, but the pain had made his brain go blank. Or maybe that was the electricity.

This was just a rehearsal for what lay ahead. When Luis Sánchez had finished parading him before the news cameras, shit would get real.

Was he afraid? Hell, yes, he was afraid. He feared for himself but even more so for Gabriela—a woman in a house full of ruthless men. The thought of what they might do to her sickened him.

Did Ruiz believe her story?

Don't think about that. Work the problem.

He sat in a wooden chair, his ankles bound to its legs, his arms twisted and tied behind his back, the ropes tight. There was no way to work himself free with *sicarios* watching him the entire time. He'd only succeed in giving himself rope burns.

The room he was in had no windows and only one door. There was a large sink to one side, chairs scattered here and there. A fucking meat hook and chains hung from the ceiling. There were tools on a nearby bench—knives, an ax, a hammer and nails, a chainsaw, a drill, pliers, a blowtorch. The tile floor had a drain, proof that this room had been built for one purpose.

Torturing and killing people was messy work.

There were five *sicarios*—all armed. They'd taken his backpack, his rifle, and his concealed pistol, leaving him with nothing. He had aced combatives—military hand-to-hand combat training—but he had no doubt these bastards would shoot him if he somehow got free of this chair and started throwing kicks and punches.

He would wait, and he would take it—whatever they did to him.

The door opened and shut, taking all sound with it, something he hadn't noticed before. Was the room soundproofed? It must be. Would it drown out the sound of gunshots, too? He would love to find out.

Acne Man was back. "Don Sergio says we have to leave him be for now, but that doesn't mean we can't have a little fun with him. Wake him up."

That was interesting news.

Someone slapped Dylan's cheek.

He opened his eyes, raised his head, but said nothing.

Acne Man pulled up a chair, spoke in Spanish. "I know you can understand me, asshole. I went up to see what the Boss wants me to do with you, but he was too busy fucking your whore of a nun. From the way she was moaning, I'd say she likes it, too."

Dylan fixed a bored expression on his face, bit his tongue. He didn't believe a word of it. The bastard wasn't a good liar. It was clear that violence was the only skill in their interrogation arsenal. Without permission to tear him apart, they had nothing.

Acne Man didn't give up, his descriptions of the action upstairs getting more extreme as he went on. Ruiz was fucking Gabriela. He had promised her to his men and then to his dogs—if there was anything left of her.

Dylan's refusal to speak stole the bastard's control, his pitted face turning a mottled shade of red as Dylan remained silent.

"I don't like the way you look at me, you fucking asshole." He drove his fist into Dylan's gut, pain forcing the breath from Dylan's lungs.

"I thought Don Sergio said to leave him be for now?"

"Someone has to teach him a lesson." Acne Man rolled his electroshock toy close again, took the homemade paddles into his hands, and flipped the switch. "I won't kill him, but I won't let him sit there laughing at us either."

He touched the paddles to Dylan's skin. Electrical current rushed through Dylan's body in a jolt of liquid agony.

STILL HUDDLED IN THE BLANKET, Gabriela finished her meal, forcing herself to swallow despite the butterflies that churned restlessly in her stomach. Outside, the storm had all but spent itself. She'd overheard Ruiz telling his men that Luis Sánchez was in the air again and would arrive soon.

She was running out of time.

She needed to reach Dylan and set him free. The two of them together had a much better chance against Ruiz and all his men than she did alone. But how could she possibly get to him? They would see her going down the stairs. And what would she do when she got there—knock on the door and ask the bad guys to let Dylan go?

The moment she pulled the trigger, the *sicarios* on the veranda would stream through the door to protect their boss, and she would be overwhelmed. She had only enough rounds in the Glock to take down fifteen of them—and that was if every shot hit its mark and was lethal. That never happened in the real world. She would need one of their weapons, preferably an rifle with spare magazines.

And how are you going to get that?

Despair gnawed at her, doubt and hopelessness sliding over her like a shadow.

What if she tried to rescue Dylan and got the two of them killed? What if she made the decision to act now and failed when a better chance would have come along later? What if it was already too late, and there was nothing she could do?

Stop! Just stop it!

She had years of HUMINT and intel training. Dylan was a special operations veteran. They were among the best-trained operatives in the US. Washington was counting on them to get out of the country without leaving proof that they'd been here. She needed to act, not waste time worrying.

She sent up a prayer to God, the Blessed Virgin, and St. Anthony and finished her meal, carefully tucking the knife into her pocket. "Thank you, Imelda. The arepas were delicious. They remind me of my grandmother's."

"*Gracias, Hermana.*"

Gabriela carried her plate to the sink, intending to wash it, but Imelda took it.

"You are a guest of Don Sergio. That is my job."

"May God bless you." Gabriela gave the cook a saintly smile. "Can you tell me where the bathroom is? I need to wash."

What she needed was an excuse to meander around the hacienda.

Imelda stepped out of the kitchen and pointed to a long hallway with marble floors. "It's the first door on your right. There are towels, too."

Gabriela walked to the bathroom, where she washed the worst of the mud away. She dried her face, her gaze meeting its twin in the mirror.

You can do this, Gabriela. You must *do this.*

Shouts. Men's voices.

She peeked out the bathroom window, saw *sicarios* running from the veranda to parked vehicles. She counted ten men. They climbed inside and drove away.

Where were they going?

The whir of a helicopter overhead answered that question. Sánchez' helicopter was going to land nearby, and they were going to meet him.

This is your chance.

She set her fear aside, wrapped the blanket around herself, and drew the Glock from her waistband, keeping it hidden. Then she stepped out of the bathroom and walked without hesitation toward Ruiz's office.

The door was open, one *sicario* on guard outside, another sitting across from Ruiz, rifle between his knees.

She put on a meek expression. "May I speak with Señor Ruiz? I do not wish to disturb him, but I remembered something he will wish to know."

The *sicario* turned. "The nun wishes—"

"I heard her, idiot. Show her in."

"Thank you." Gabriela went to stand behind the seated

sicario and across from Ruiz, pretending that she wasn't terrified. "Señor, pardon me, but I just remembered..."

She let the blanket fall away, pointed the weapon at Ruiz. "I'm not a nun."

She fired.

Pop! Pop!

The *sicario* at the door raised his rifle, but Gabriela was faster, taking him out first, and then shooting the man who had jumped to his feet in front of her.

Pop! Pop!

Shouts from the veranda.

A scream.

Imelda.

Shit!

Gabriela grabbed both *sicarios'* rifles, dashed out of the office, and ran up the stairs on the opposite side of the foyer, positioning herself as best she could for cover—and a good view of the entrance below. She raised up the rifle just as men rushed through the door, heading for Ruiz's office.

She pulled the trigger.

Nothing.

The fire selector!

She flicked the switch from safe to full-auto and poured on the fire.

Ratatatatatatatatat!

One down.

But firing a fully automatic weapon was new to her. She wasn't prepared for the way the recoil forced the muzzle to rise, moving her off-target.

Now the others knew where she was.

They turned, shouted at her, raised their rifles.

She fired again, going for three-round bursts and trying

to be methodical, taking out the one aiming at her first before firing at the next.

Ratatat! Ratatat! Ratatat!

Two down. Three. Four.

Ratatat! Ratatat! Ratatat!

They returned fire, plaster exploding from the wall around her, something hot slicing across her ribcage.

Ratatat! Ratatat! Ratatat!

Silence.

Below her, the marble floor of the foyer was red with blood.

Rifle raised, she waited, certain the men who were with Dylan would have heard the gunfire and would come running upstairs to help. But they didn't.

She walked carefully down the stairs, watching for movement among the bodies on the floor. She checked them, one by one, to make sure they were dead, then walked into Ruiz's office.

Sergio de Anda Ruiz, the leader of the Andes Cartel, sat in his chair, face on his desk, most definitely dead, two bullet holes in his head, the back of his skull blown away.

She grabbed a set of car keys from his desk and took another man's rifle, checking to make sure the magazine was full. Then she made her way down the back stairs, knowing that the other *sicarios* would return soon—and that Luis Sánchez and the media would be with them.

I'm coming, Dylan.

18

Dylan fought to catch his breath, shredded by the blinding pain of another electroshock.

God, how about that miracle? Please.

Was he praying?

Acne Man bent down, got in his face, his breath reeking of alcohol. "Are you from the US, a gringo? Answer me!"

But Dylan must have been hallucinating, because in that instant the door opened, and Gabriela stepped into the room like something out of a video game fantasy, carrying an Israeli IWI Tavor. She opened fire.

Ratatat! Ratatat! Ratatat! Ratatat!

The noise was deafening.

Fuck!

Was this *real*?

As quickly as it began, it was over, blood running across the floor and trickling down the drain.

Then she was there, cutting the ropes that bound him. "I'm so sorry, Dylan. I got here as fast as I could. Hey, Dylan, are you with me?"

"Yeah." He tried to pull himself together.

"Are you going to be able to walk?"

"Yeah, I'm good." He stood—and sagged against her. "Give me a minute."

"We need to get out of here—now. The men who left to get Sánchez will be back at any minute. We should find your backpack, too. It's in Ruiz's office."

Dylan's brain must have been fried because he couldn't seem to grasp what she was telling him. "My shirt. My boots. I'm going to need them."

She gathered them and grabbed a rifle off one of the men she'd just killed for him. "Here—and hurry! Ten of Ruiz's men went to pick up Sánchez. If they get back before we're gone, this night is going to get a lot bloodier."

Dylan sat in one of the other chairs, put on his boots, T-shirt, and ACU shirt, the pieces beginning to come together. "You said ten of his men went to get Sánchez. What about the others?"

"They're dead. I shot them." She glanced around. "What kind of hellhole is this?"

"You shot them *all*?" He stared at her.

Seriously, his brain had to be completely fucking fried.

"They were torturing you, Dylan. They were going to kill you. What else could I do?" She held the Tavor at the ready, looked up the stairs.

"Yeah. Right." Then he saw. "You're bleeding."

Blood soaked the side of her T-shirt.

"Just a graze. We can deal with it later. We need to go."

Dylan checked his rifle and followed Gabriela up the stairs, training kicking in, clearing his mind. The house was dead silent. When they reached the top of the stairs, he saw she wasn't kidding. Dead *sicarios* lay on top of each other in the foyer, blood everywhere, the wall pocked with bullet holes.

¡Ay, virgen santa! Oh, Holy Virgin!

"Your backpack is in there."

He followed her into what must have been Ruiz's office to see Ruiz himself dead where he sat, brains blown out. "*¡Coño!* You killed the head of the Andes Cartel."

"I had no choice."

"No, you didn't." Dylan grabbed his backpack, checked it, found his phone and the first aid kit inside. He handed the first aid kit to her. "You'll need this. Hang onto it. What's the plan?"

"I don't have one. I've been making this up. I say we steal a vehicle and get out of here now. I took these keys off Ruiz's desk. Or maybe you think we should try to steal the helicopter?"

"I sure as hell don't know how to fly a chopper. Do you?"

"No." She glanced toward the back window, a hint of panic in her voice. "See the headlights? That's them. They're coming back."

Dylan put on his helmet with his NVGs flipped up and then shouldered his pack. "We need to create a diversion, pin his men down."

"How do we do that?"

"You stay here. I'll be right back." He ran into the kitchen, found a woman crouched down and crying.

Son of a bitch!

They couldn't afford to leave witnesses behind. Whoever this woman was, she'd probably seen Gabriela kill Ruiz and his men. Now she'd seen Dylan's face. But he couldn't bring himself to kill her.

"Auntie, I won't hurt you, but you need to run. This house is going to explode and burn. Is there anyone else here, anyone still alive?"

"N-no." She stared at him in horror then fled out the back door.

He dropped to his knees, took a breaching charge out of his backpack, and stuck it to the stove. He carefully set up the fuse and rigged the detonator. Then he opened the oven door and turned on the gas, taking the detonator with him.

"How do we know which vehicle these keys belong to?"

Dylan took the keys on the run, looked at the logo. "We're searching for a Land Rover. We've got to go—now."

He lowered his NVGs, ran down the front steps, saw no sign of anyone, no glowing green shapes of human beings.

Behind them, the sound of engines drew closer.

They ran to the Land Rover, Gabriella clutching her side.

"Why don't you let me drive this time?" He hopped into the driver's seat, stuck the keys in the ignition, and started the engine but didn't turn on the lights.

Gabriela climbed into her seat, looked back over her shoulder. "They're coming."

A half dozen headlights drove toward the hacienda, coming up some backroad that probably led to a private airport or helipad.

"It's okay." He reached over, took her hand, found it clammy. *Shit.* "They don't know we're in the vehicle, and they're about to be very busy."

He held up the detonator, pushed the button.

BLAM!

Hacienda Ruiz went up like a fireball.

With the headlights still off, Dylan drove down the driveway and out of the gate, leaving the burning hacienda behind them.

∾

"Do you know what you did back there?"

"I rescued us." Gabriela pressed a blood-clotting trauma bandage against the wound in her side, the pain sharp, the momentary rush of elation she'd felt as they'd driven away replaced by a strange sense of ... numbness.

"You also singlehandedly killed one of the most-wanted bastards in the world and twelve of his *sicarios*. What happened?"

Gabriela told him the whole story, words pouring out of her in a rush as she got to the part with the shooting, the whole thing like a dream. "I shot Ruiz and the two others with the Glock, then grabbed a guy's rifle but forgot to switch the fire selector to auto, and so the others knew where I was before I was able to fire. The rifle was heavy, and the muzzle kept wanting to point at the ceiling, but I tried hard to hold onto it. I thought the guys torturing you would hear despite the soundproofing, but they didn't, so I went straight down and opened the door. You know the rest."

He reached over, rested a hand on her shoulder. "That took guts, Gabriela. You saved our lives. You're one in a million."

"I guess so."

He glanced over at her, his brow furrowed. "How are you feeling?"

She started to tremble. "N-not so well at the moment."

Dylan pulled off the road, parked, and flicked on the cabin light. "Lift the bandage. Let me see it."

Confusion muddled her thoughts. "S-see what?"

He reached out, lifted the bandage, his voice soft, comforting. "The clotting agent is working. The bleeding has stopped. You're right that it's just a graze, but it's a deep one. There might be bullet fragments in there. You're going to need stitches."

"Okay." What was wrong with her?

He pressed the bandage back into place, put her hand on it. "The adrenaline is wearing off. I think you're in a kind of post-combat shock."

"Post-combat shock? That's lame." She wasn't supposed to be weak.

He cupped her cheek. "It's a normal reaction. I've seen it in new SEALs back from their first real combat mission. They're trained to fight. You're not."

That made her feel a little better. "I don't want to be a wimp."

"God, woman, you're anything but a wimp. When we get to a stopping point, I'll treat your wound, and you can get some sleep."

"Wait! I'm going to be sick." She unbuckled her seatbelt, opened the door, hopped to the ground—and lost her supper in the grass.

Then Dylan was there, stroking her hair, handing her a bottle of water. "It's okay, Gabi. Just get it out of your system. You're going to be all right."

"Sorry." Throwing up in front of a lover had never been high on her bucket list.

"Hey, don't apologize. You deserve a fucking medal." He helped her to her feet and back into the Land Rover and climbed into the driver's seat once again.

Lights. Sirens.

He pulled deeper into the trees.

Firetrucks. National police. *Guachimanes.*

When they had gone, he drove back onto the road, heading for the main highway.

Then it occurred to Gabriela. "Where are we going?"

"We can't drive around in that bastard's Land Rover for long. As soon as his men discover it's missing, they'll try to track it. A high-end vehicle like this has anti-theft technology for sure. So, I'm heading back to where we left the Aveo. If it's still there, we'll switch."

"But we can't drive across the border."

"We're not crossing into Colombia—not with fucking drones patrolling the sky." He turned on the Land Rover's headlights as they reached the main highway. "We're heading north."

"North?" There was nothing up there but the Caribbean.

He's a SEAL.

Shit.

"Don't worry about that now. I need you to help me navigate back to the Aveo."

Gabriela fought to pull herself together. "The easiest way to retrace our path would probably be to head up the highway and get off at that same exit."

"Do you remember which exit that was? You were driving."

She nodded. "I think so."

Having a task seemed to focus her mind. Her body stopped trembling, her numbness falling away as she watched for the correct exit.

There were no roadblocks to slow them, but it was midnight by the time they found the Aveo. They backtracked the way they'd come and drove toward San Cristóbal, avoiding the city itself and heading north toward Maracaibo.

Then she had to ask. "How do you do it? How do you go into combat and then move on with your life as if nothing happened?"

He took her hand, squeezed it. "You don't."

LUIS STARED AT THE FLAMES, stunned. He climbed out of his vehicle just as another explosion rocked the place, the heat so extreme he could feel it even at this distance. "What ... What has happened?"

"*Jefe*, please get back inside." Mono tried to herd him back into the vehicle. "This is dangerous. We don't know what has happened or whether the men who did this are still here."

Behind him, cameras clicked.

The reporters.

The bitch from Globovisión stepped in front of the camera. "We're standing near the home of Colombian businessman Sergio Ruiz, which is in flames. We can't confirm whether Ruiz was inside at the time or whether there are fatalities—"

Luis rounded on her. "Turn it off! Turn the fucking cameras off!"

He hadn't brought them here to broadcast his failure.

Mono walked over, ripped the mic out of her hand. "You heard Don Luis. Put your cameras away."

Jeronimo Ruiz, Sergio's younger cousin, who'd met them at the helipad, walked up to Luis, tears on his face. "My cousin was in that house. This must be a hit by one of the other cartels. We'll find whoever did this and make them watch while we do the same to their families."

Luis found the bastard's tears repulsive. "It's not a cartel, idiot. It's the US commando. He did this."

Jeronimo glared at him. "You'd better hope not. He was here because you asked for Don Sergio's help. If he did this, then it is *your* fault, Don Luis."

"How can it be my fault?" Luis laughed. "Your cousin's men had charge of the bastard. If he overcame them—"

Jeronimo got in his face. "There is no way one man, stripped of his gear and tied to a chair, could overcome *all* of those men. Or maybe you think the little nun did this?"

Luis' pulse skipped. The bastard was crazy. "No, of course, not."

"The commando and nun are dead, just like my cousin." Jeronimo backed off, wiped the tears from his face. "This is the work of those Gulf bastards."

One of the other men ran up to Jeronimo. "The fire department and police are almost here."

What good would that do? The hacienda was destroyed. There probably wouldn't even be identifiable bodies. If this were the work of the Gulf Cartel, they had destroyed his proof that US special forces took the hostages. The prize he'd hoped to give his brother-in-law might be ashes.

"*Mamagüevo!*" Luis cursed, stomped a boot into the ground.

"Look!" someone shouted. "It's Imelda!"

Imelda? Sergio's cook?

She ran toward them in her white cook's uniform, hysterical and crying. "*¡Ayúdenme! ¡Ayúdenme!*" *Help me!*

Jeronimo walked over to her, took her hand. "You're safe, woman. Tell me what happened. This was the Gulf Cartel, wasn't it?"

"No, señor. It was that demon, the one pretending to be a nun. She shot Don Sergio. Then she killed them all. I was so scared."

Jeronimo laughed. "The little nun?"

"*Sí.* Then she went down and freed *him*, the man they brought in with her. He warned me that he was going to blow up the house and told me to run."

Luis stepped in. "Did he speak English?"

"No, señor, he spoke Spanish. They both spoke only Spanish."

Jeronimo gave Imelda a shake. "You saw the nun kill my cousin?"

"I was in the kitchen, but I heard it. But she cannot be a nun. She is a demon."

Jeronimo released Imelda and turned to Luis, rage on his ugly face. He pointed to the helicopter. "Take your reporters and get the fuck out of here! You brought this down on us. You're lucky I don't gut you where you stand!"

Mono and his men raised their rifles, pointed them at Jeronimo's men.

"No, Mono, lower your weapon. They are grieving. We will talk again soon, Jeronimo. I'm sorry about Don Sergio. He was a good friend."

That wasn't true, but it wasn't right to speak ill of the dead.

"Mono, get the reporters back into the vehicles. Call the pilot and tell him to prepare to lift off. We're going back to Caracas."

But Jeronimo wasn't finished. "We will find your commando and this demon nun, and we'll deal with them our way. They are ours now. Our partnership with you is over. You are no longer a friend of the Andes organization."

Luis' stomach seemed to drop, blood rushing from his head. "Our partnership—"

"It's over!" Jeronimo spat on the ground.

His partnership with Sergio and the cartel was the source of his wealth—and his brother-in-law's most significant secret source of income. Without it...

His brother-in-law would kill him. "We can discuss this at another time. You're upset, I know, and we grieve with..."

Jeronimo drew a pistol, pressed it against Luis' forehead. "Leave! Now!"

"Don Luis, please, get in the vehicle," Mono said.

Luis climbed inside, fear a weight in his belly as they drove back to the helipad.

19

Dylan drove toward Maracaibo, Gabriela asleep in the seat beside him, her face lined with exhaustion and worry. Or was that pain?

She'd come so fucking close to being killed today.

They both had.

If someone had told him at the initial mission briefing that the nun would turn out to be a CIA officer and would not only provide valuable intel, but also take out a dozen killers along with the head of the Andes Cartel, Dylan would have thought they were loco. And yet, she'd done all those things—and more.

It was supposed to be Dylan's job to keep her safe, but she had risked herself to save him. She'd never killed before, but today she'd taken the lives of thirteen men, something she would carry with her for the rest of her life. She had a higher kill count than he did for this mission, and *she* was the one being rescued.

But that wasn't the crazy part.

The crazy part was that he was falling in love with her.

¡Coño!

If that was true, he was fucked.

Whatever he was feeling, it was probably just adrenaline getting mixed up with hormones. He was a man, and she was a beautiful, smart, talented, courageous, brilliant, sexy woman. Once they got back to the US, they'd go their separate ways and ...

And he didn't want that.

Tough shit, cabrón. *She's got her life, her career. Do you think she'd give it up for a man who couldn't keep her safe?*

Dylan had replayed the past eight hours over and over in his mind, trying to figure out what he'd done wrong. But it all came back to one thing: drones. That was the crucial missing piece of intel. If he'd known about the drones, he would have headed north rather than trying to cross the Colombian border.

Wasn't that the sort of shit the Agency ought to have known?

Beside him, Gabriela whimpered in her sleep—then jerked awake.

Dylan took her hand. "It's okay, Gabi. You're safe."

She pressed a palm against her side, pain on her face. "Where are we?"

"We just passed a sign that said Arincón. It shouldn't be long now. You've slept for about two hours."

"Sorry. I should be doing something useful."

"You've done enough."

They pulled into Maracaibo just after sunrise. Dylan checked them into a cheap motel just off the highway—no security cameras, no elevators, no questions asked. The room wasn't fancy, but it was clean and had a private bathroom and AC.

Gabriela took off her blood-stained shirt and jeans. "I want a shower."

"You can wash your hands and face, but no shower—not for at least twenty-four hours. That wound needs time to heal first." He set his backpack down. "I'll give you some morphine, clean it, and stitch you up."

"Morphine?"

"Believe me. It will be better that way."

She washed her hands and face and set her bloody T-shirt and jeans in the sink to soak. "I think I'm going to need new clothes."

Dylan laid a towel across the bed and got what he needed from the first aid kit—gloves, sterile tweezers, suture kit, morphine. "Get comfortable."

"Have you ever done this before?"

"I trained to be our Team's back-up medic, and the answer is yes."

"Is it going to be bad?" She lay down, centering herself over the towel.

Dylan put a pillow beneath her head. "I have to remove the bullet fragments, or you'll get an infection. That's what the morphine is for."

She watched him, clearly nervous. "I trust you."

He twisted the top off the auto-injector. "This is going to make you feel sleepy and light-headed. It won't take all the pain away, but it will help. Ready?"

She nodded.

He punched the auto-injector into her quadriceps.

She gasped at the prick, and then her eyes went wide.

She reached for him. "Dylan?"

He took her hand. "It's just the drug. Have you ever had morphine before?"

"Never. It feels ... so strange."

"I'm going to wash my hands now while it kicks in. I'll be

right back." He walked into the bathroom, turned on the tap, reached for an unopened bar of soap.

"Dylan? Will I see you again after we get home? You can't just pop into my life like this and then disappear. I don't want to say goodbye."

His pulse picked up. "I don't want that either."

Part of Dylan wondered if he would come to regret saying that, but it was the truth. Then again, she was on ten mgs of morphine. She probably wouldn't remember this conversation anyway.

He dried his hands, slipped into sterile gloves, and opened the tweezers. "I'm going to get the bullet fragments now. Try to hold still."

Her lips curved in a dopey smile. "Okey-dokey."

He worked quickly, trying not to hurt her, but, of course, that was impossible. The drug blunted her pain, but her every gasp and whimper was a fist to his solar plexus. He removed three fragments, rinsed the wound, and sutured it, causing her more pain. Then he cleaned her skin with some sterile saline and bandaged her. "How are you?"

She watched him through dilated pupils, a sheen of perspiration on her forehead, her face pale. "As good as new. I really can't take a shower? I feel so dirty."

Dylan had an idea. "I can give you a sponge bath."

"A sponge bath?"

"You'll see." He cleaned up the mess and put away the first aid kit, then grabbed the room's ice bucket and carried it into the bathroom. He filled it with hot water and grabbed the soap and a washcloth.

He found her naked on the bed, drowsy but still awake. He set the bucket down on the nightstand, soaked the washcloth, and started with her face.

"Mmm. That feels good."

He moved his way down her body, washing away proof of the day's cruelty——blood spatter, dust from the drywall, mud from the river. Every inch of her was precious to him, her body sacred ground. Her throat. Her shoulders. Her breasts. Her belly. The curve of her hips. Those slender legs. Her little feet.

Yeah, he was in deep shit.

He set the dirty cloth in the ice bucket. "Is that better?"

She nodded. "I'm so sleepy."

He kissed her. "Just rest. I'm going to take a quick shower."

He covered her with the sheet, double-checked the door, and walked into the bathroom with his pistol. When he stepped out of the bathroom once more, towel around his waist, she was deep in a painless sleep.

GABRIELA LAY on her good side next to Dylan, tracing a finger down the groove at the center of his belly, her body replete from sex—very slow, careful, gentle sex. "What a pair we make. You're bruised and battered. I've got stitches."

Dark bruises covered his chest and ribcage, and there were blotchy red marks on his belly where that son of a bitch had shocked him.

Dylan's eyes were closed, but he smiled. "I've been worse off. Believe me."

"That place looked like a butcher shop. It must have been awful." She placed her palm over the red marks.

His brow furrowed, his smile fading. "I've never felt pain like that—ever. Nothing even comes close. I had to hold out because, if I'd broken, they would have killed you. I thought of you, Gabriela. The whole time, I thought of you. I even prayed and asked God for a miracle. And then you were there with that Tavor."

Tears filled Gabriela's eyes, an ache in her chest to think of him suffering like that. Then she had to say it. "I'm so sorry, Dylan. If I hadn't let myself get washed downstream—"

"Hey, it wasn't your fault." He sat up, took her face between his palms, his eyes looking straight into hers. "They knew right where we were when I shot down that drone. They probably flew another one into position and watched us cross. They would have been waiting for us no matter where we came out of the river. You didn't get us into that mess, but you sure as hell got us out of it."

His fingers slid into her hair, and he kissed her, soft and slow. "You are the best mission I've ever had."

Gabriela saw a ray of hope in his words. She slid a palm up his chest, gathered her courage. "I don't want this to end."

He looked confused. "You want to keep running from the bad guys forever?"

"No, I don't want *this* to end—you and me."

He grinned, chuckled. "I know. You told me last night."

"I... I did?"

"The morphine loosened your tongue a little."

"Oh." Heat rushed to her face.

"Before we start worrying about the future, how about we make sure we actually have one? We still have a long way to go to get home."

Just like that, he switched from being tender to discussing business.

"I'm going to head out for some food and clothes for the two of us." He climbed out of bed and dressed, his trousers as filthy as her clothes but not bloodstained. "You hang here. Keep the curtains closed. Don't go out. When I get back, we'll eat, and then take off."

"I wear a size six." He hadn't asked, but he would need to know. "Where exactly are we going?"

"I'm working on that." He grabbed his sunglasses, his pistol, and the car keys, then pressed a kiss to her nose. "Size six. Got it. Don't open the door for anyone."

"Hurry back."

"I'll do my best." He unlocked the door, stepped outside, and was gone.

Gabriela wrapped herself in the sheet, then washed her face, brushed her teeth, and turned on the television. She had expected to find news of Ruiz's death, but there was nothing about him or the fire at his hacienda on any of the channels. Why would anyone want to keep that a secret?

The moment she asked the question, she knew the answer.

His death had created a power vacuum. The top position in one of the world's wealthiest crime organizations was open. Someone didn't want anyone to know Ruiz was dead —not until he had secured his position and taken that power for himself.

With any luck, the cartel was too busy killing its own to come after them.

Have you been lucky so far?

No. Except for Dylan.

He'd come after her when Pitón had tried to take her for himself. He'd done everything he could to keep her safe, enduring far more than he'd signed on for with this mission. He'd picked lead out of her and stitched her up.

He'd made love to her like no man ever had.

That doesn't mean he loves you.

Of course, it didn't.

When she'd brought up the future, he'd changed the subject. He was right. Now wasn't the time or place. But she couldn't shake the worry that this was nothing more than a fling for him. Which completely sucked.

She was in love with him.

God, she was an idiot!

She was on her first solo mission, and she just *had* to fall in love with the first sexy former SEAL to come along and rescue her.

Well done.

Then her face appeared on the TV screen.

"Police continue to search for Sister María Catalina, who was abducted from a Mission in El Vigía. In a twist, police believe she and the man she is traveling with may have been responsible for the murders of thirteen men near San Antonio del Táchira last night. More on this story as it develops."

How would they know any of that? How would they—

Imelda.

Of course. The cook. Gabriela had heard her scream. She'd seen.

¡Mierda! Shit.

Sánchez and his men were still looking for her. The cartel would be coming for her, too. And they knew now that she wasn't a nun.

"You want to steal a boat? *That's* your plan?"

"Or rent or borrow one." Dylan tried not to notice how fucking hot she looked in the red tank top and jeans he'd bought for her. "I don't think I can buy one for five hundred bucks—not one that will get us safely to Curaçao anyway."

They had finished their late lunch—arepas stuffed with pork, cheese, and rice—and they needed to hit the road. He'd stolen some plates off a car, switching them for the plates on the Aveo, hoping to keep the police off their tail.

"Have you figured out how we're going to get through the maritime border? The cartel is out there, too, along with the Venezuelan navy. Don't forget that the navy threatened to fire on a civilian ship loaded with food and medical supplies from *your* island just to save face."

Dylan hadn't forgotten. "I'll take my chances against them on the open water over drones and dickheads in the jungle."

"You're going all SEAL on me, aren't you? Remember the river. I can't hold my breath for an hour or swim like a dolphin."

"Neither can I." He chuckled, sat on the bed beside her, took her hand and kissed it. "This is our best bet for getting out of here. Trust me."

"I do."

"The question is, where do we go to get the boat."

She considered that. "Coro. It's got a decent harbor. It's only forty miles from there to Curaçao. There are lots of boats—and lots of men willing to make a run to Curaçao for a price."

"Human traffickers?"

"Yes. It's a sketchy scene. People have been held for ransom. Others have been put on boats that aren't seaworthy and have drowned."

"Good to know." He'd be on the alert. "If we leave now, we can make it to Curaçao before nightfall."

They headed out, taking the bridge across Lake Maracaibo and heading toward Coro, Gabriela navigating with a paper map he'd bought from the motel. Compared to the twists and turns of the roads around San Cristóbal, the highway to Coro was almost a straight line. There were no roadblocks, perhaps because everyone thought they were trying to cross into Colombia. But that was one lesson he'd learned as a SEAL.

Never do what the enemy expects you to do.

It was only a three-and-a-half-hour drive to Coro, and it passed quickly, the two of them sharing stories from growing up—Dylan's fascination with sharks, Gabriela's desire to be a ballerina and then a gymnast and then a figure skater.

"You would look cute in a pink tutu," Dylan said.

"Oh, you have no idea."

"I can sure as hell imagine it."

It was late afternoon when they pulled into Coro. Dylan stepped out of the vehicle, inhaled the scent of the sea. "Can you smell it?"

"The arepas?"

That made Dylan laugh. "What is your obsession with arepas? I meant the sea."

It smelled like home.

While Gabriela waited in the car, Dylan spoke with a couple of locals about how best to hire someone to take them across. Both told him to go to the cantina closest to the pier and let the men there know what he wanted. That seemed like a bad idea to Dylan, but he wasn't going to find someone by googling on his phone.

"I should go in with you."

"No way. Someone might recognize you."

"You're too scary-looking with all those muscles. No one's going to want to take you on. If I'm with you..."

"No." He parked the car, kissed her cheek, and got out.

Inside, the cantina was busy with men who drank and

smoked—and who completely ignored him when he told the bartender in a loud voice that he was willing to pay the right person good money in US dollars for a boat ride to Curaçao.

Then the place fell silent, every man's gaze shifting to the door.

There stood Gabriela, doing that thing she did, exuding sensuality from every pore. She crossed to the bar, slid her arm through Dylan's. "Rum and Coke, please."

The bartender, a big bald man, almost fell over himself getting her drink.

"Whiskey for me." Dylan nuzzled her cheek. "I told you to stay in the car."

"Have you found a boat yet?" She sipped her drink then gave the bartender that smile of hers, the one that made Dylan weak. "My husband and I are looking for someone to take us to Curaçao this afternoon. Can you help us?"

The bartender leaned forward, lowered his voice. "You don't want any of these men to take you, Señora. My cousin has just the boat you need."

"Call him. We'd like to meet him—now."

Twenty minutes later, Dylan found himself walking along the pier with Gabriela and Paulito, a former navy man whose weathered skin proved that he'd spent much of his life on the water. "Is the boat seaworthy?"

"Sí, and very fast, too." Paulito clearly loved his boat. "The maritime border is closed, so it's going to cost you more. We could be stopped or boarded."

"We stop for no one. Is that clear?"

"That could get tricky."

"I have a few skills up my sleeve. Name your price."

"A thousand dollars US."

Dylan didn't have that. "I can pay you five hundred now and a thousand when we reach Curaçao."

Paulito studied him, hands on his hips. "You must really need to get out of here. Are you in some kind of trouble?"

"Do you want the money or not? Show me the boat."

"This way."

Most of the boats here had wooden hulls and looked like they'd break apart in choppy water. And then he saw it.

"There she is." Paulito chuckled. "Isn't she pretty?"

Dylan couldn't help but smile. "She is a beauty."

The boat was a refitted RHIB—a rigid-hulled inflatable boat—similar to the ones that the Teams used. He knew these boats inside and out and could pilot it himself. He could even work on the engine in a pinch.

"So, now it's a deal?"

Dylan met Gabriela's gaze and gave her a nod. "*Sí,* Paulito, it's a deal."

20

Gabriela took Dylan's hand, accepted his help stepping up and onto the boat, which rocked beneath their weight.

Dylan chuckled. "It's not going to flip over."

Paulito bent down, untied the rope from a piling. "The water can get choppy. Do either of you get seasick?"

"Nah, man, I'm good."

But Gabriela had no idea. "I guess we'll find out."

Paulito grinned. "Have you ever been on a boat?"

"No. I think I prefer dry land."

Dylan led her to the center of the small craft, where there were three rows of benches, each with a handrail in front of it. "When we get up to speed, you'll need to hold onto this."

"Back in the day, I used to take tourists on excursions along the coast and to Aruba and Curaçao. My boat would be full—five trips a day." With the boat free of its pilings, Paulito climbed on board and headed for the cabin. "Now, there are no tourists. I take whoever can pay me."

"I'm sorry, Paulito." Gabriela felt sorry for him, and yet

he was one of millions who'd lost their livelihoods. So many lives changed, so many ruined, so many lost. "Let us hope things change soon."

He started the motor and began to pilot the craft away from the pier.

Dylan knelt beside her, spoke for her ears only. "I've turned my phone on and notified Cobra of our location and heading. They'll be tracking us now. If we run into trouble, you take shelter in the cabin."

"Where will you be?"

"Shooting back." He kissed her, stood. "Let's go."

Gabriela watched the water glide by then looked up at the distant hills that surrounded the harbor. All at once, it hit her—she was leaving Venezuela.

Heart breaking, she stood, made her way to the stern of the boat, looked back toward Coro, her throat tight, tears filling her eyes. The sob caught her by surprise, and she covered her mouth to stifle it.

A hand came to rest against her lower back.

"Are you okay?"

She shook her head. "I was so focused on escaping that it didn't dawn on me until now. I'm leaving a country I love, and I don't think I'll ever be able to return. You should have seen it before, Dylan. It wasn't perfect, but life was good. But now ... I never got to visit my Abuelita Isabel's grave."

He drew her against him, kissed her hair, held her while she wept. "I'm so sorry, Gabi. Maybe one day, things will be different."

"Is your wife okay?" Paulito called back to them.

"She's fine." Dylan stepped back, wiped the tears from her face, his eyes looking into hers. "We're about to leave the shelter of the harbor. You might want to sit."

A heaviness in her chest, she walked back to the bench

and sat, a stiff breeze blowing through her hair as the boat gained speed.

Dylan stood off to the side, his gaze on what lay ahead of them. "We're coming up on some six-foot swells. The boat's going to start bouncing, so hold on."

She was about to ask what he meant by *bounce* when the boat did just that—once, twice, three times. She grabbed the bar, held on. "That's not so bad."

"Listen to you. Already a pro." Dylan grinned, looking as handsome as sin in his new black T-shirt and jeans. Somehow, he managed to keep his footing without holding onto anything. He was in his environment, a SEAL finally back at sea.

The thought made her smile.

Then her heart, which was already hurting, constricted.

In a little more than an hour, they'd be in Curaçao, and this would be over. She'd just said goodbye to Venezuela, and soon she would say goodbye to Dylan.

You knew this would happen.

Yes, but that didn't make it easy.

They moved along the coast for a while, Dylan talking with Paulito in the cabin. Venezuela was still a shadow on the horizon, fishing vessels coming home with the day's catch, a lone oil tanker heading toward Cuba. Then Paulito turned the prow north, and they headed out into open water, picking up speed.

Whump! Whump! Whump!

The boat seemed to bounce over the waves, landing hard on the water. Or was that concrete? No, it was water.

Dylan stood outside the cabin, holding on with one hand, his feet wide apart as he kept watch for navy patrol vessels.

He shouted, pointed. "On the port beam!"

Gabriela followed the direction of his gaze and saw it—a small vessel flying the ensign of the Venezuelan Navy.

DYLAN WATCHED the patrol ship that now sat dead astern, riding their wake, matching their pace, following them. He didn't like this at all. He tapped out a quick message to Tower. "Why aren't they trying to board us?"

"I don't know."

If they had been planning to board, the ship would have caught up with them by now and ordered them to stop. Instead, the vessel hung back, watching, following. Were they waiting for something—another ship, a helicopter perhaps?

Using Paulito's binoculars, Dylan watched both the sea and sky, listening for the heavy thrum of helicopter rotors, misgiving heavy in his chest.

There! And there.

They were so low in the water he'd almost missed them.

"Two cigarette boats coming in fast, three points aft of the starboard beam!"

"Cigarette boats?" Paulito gaped at him, face going pale. "Who the hell are you? I should have listened to my wife. I should have stayed home."

"Go full throttle!" Dylan grabbed his backpack, pulled out his rifle, checked it, flipped it into full-auto. "Gabriela, get up here!"

She stood, stumbled forward, eyes wide. "What are cigarette boats?"

"Speed boats used by cartels to evade radar." He reached for her, brought her into the shelter of the cabin. "Stay down."

He took up position astern, watched the naval vessel veer off, its job here done. So, the navy had ties to drug smugglers. Well, no surprise there.

Dylan peered through his scope, saw men with rifles—six per boat. Not Guachimanes, but men in street clothes. Ruiz's men.

Andes Cartel.

¡Hijoeputas! Sons of whores.

But how the hell had they found them?

He made his way back to the cabin—and pointed his rifle at Paulito. "How much are they paying you?"

"Dylan!"

"Gabi, stay down!"

Paulito stepped back, arms raised. "Don't kill me. You've got this wrong. I'm not working for them—whoever they are."

"Please, Dylan!" Gabriela stood. "I believe he's telling the truth!"

Dylan handed the rifle to Gabi, took the controls, bringing the RHIB up to full speed. "The two of you stay down."

"You can't outrun them, and if you try, they'll kill us all."

Paulito was right. They couldn't outrun them.

But Dylan had more experience at sea than they did. "I've know a few tricks."

He could hear their engines now. They were trying to outflank him, one to port the other to starboard. "Hang on!"

He turned sharply to port, threw the RHIB into a tight spiral, cutting directly in front of one of the cigarette boats and wrapping around behind it.

Dylan held the spiral, watched as the idiots tried at first to follow him, but at that speed, they couldn't handle it. One of the boats flipped, disgorging its crew into the sea, the second nearly colliding with the first.

Dylan chuckled, came out of the spiral, and shot forward again, checking and correcting his course.

"You're a crazy bastard!" Paulito shouted.

The second boat hesitated, its crew trying to decide whether they should rescue their comrades in the water or leave them and try to find them later. But Dylan had little doubt what they would choose. For men who killed for a living, life was cheap.

A moment later, the bastards were on their tail again.

Where the hell was a grenade launcher when you needed one? He had explosive breaching charges, but he couldn't very well ask the enemy to stop and wait for him to attach one to their boat.

Ratatat! Ratatat! Ratatat!

They opened fire, but couldn't shoot worth shit, not bouncing along on the swells.

"Gabi, I need you to take the wheel!"

"Me?" She stood, fear on her pretty face.

He gave her a quick lesson. "This is the throttle. This steers the ship. All you have to do is hold this course and speed. Can you do that?"

Ratatat! Ratatat! Ratatat!

She looked into his eyes, clearly terrified, but nodded. "Yes. Yes, I can do it."

God, he loved her.

He grabbed his rifle, crawled toward the stern, and got into position.

The other boat accelerated, rapidly gaining on them.

Dylan willed himself to relax, raised the weapon, and sighted on the pilot of the other craft. He watched, waited, adjusting for the rhythms of the waves, the beat of his pulse, the pace of his breathing.

BAM!

The man fell back, pulling the throttle with him.

The boat slowed, drifted, bobbing in the water as the remaining men on board scrambled to get the body out of the way and take over.

One *hijoeputo* down. Five to go.

He raised the rifle again, the boat far behind them now. But someone else would take the helm, and they would catch up. And he'd take that bastard out, too.

"Dylan!" Gabriela called for him. "Helicopters!"

He searched the sky, saw three white and orange AW139s flying straight toward them. He stayed low, made his way back up to the cabin, the choppers almost on them.

"What should I do?"

He grabbed the binoculars. *¡Wepa! Fuck, yes!* "Those aren't cartel helicopters. They're Dutch Caribbean Coast Guard. We're in Dutch waters now."

Gabriela sagged against him, going weak with relief, her eyes drifting shut. "Thank God and the Blessed Virgin and Saint Anthony."

Paulito stood, seeming surprised to be alive, but mad as hell. "You bastard, what will they do to me? Am I going to jail?"

"No, Paulito." Gabriela hugged him. "You're not going to jail. We're very grateful for your help. We'll make sure you get paid."

One helo hovered over them, while the other two continued toward to the cigarette boats. Then a voice came over a loudspeaker. "This is the Dutch Caribbean Coast Guard. Cut your engine and prepared to be boarded!"

"Who are you?" Paulito asked again.

Dylan cut the boat's engine. "It's better for you if you don't know."

"What happens to my family and me? The cartel will slaughter us!"

Dylan knew Paulito's fear wasn't irrational. "How would you like to relocate your family to Curaçao—or the US?"

GABRIELA SCANNED HER KEY CARD, pushed open the door to their hotel room, and stepped inside, Dylan a step behind her. She had a bag with a change of clothes in her hands, thanks to the US Consulate, which was in touch with the Pentagon and Cobra. She didn't yet have access to her bank accounts and wouldn't until she got back to Virginia.

She dropped the bag onto the floor and sat on the bed, drained both physically and emotionally. "I can't believe it's over. I kept expecting to end up dead."

Dylan lowered his battered backpack to the floor and stretched out on the bed beside her, his head propped up on an elbow. "I told you I'd get us home—but I was only able to keep that promise because of you. You saved my life. You saved your own life. You are the bravest, strongest woman I know."

Gabriela didn't see how that could be true. "I don't think I've ever been more afraid than when I recognized Ruiz. I was sure he would kill us then and there. And today, when I saw those cigarette boats..." She'd known it had to be the cartel. "What you did, outmaneuvering them on the water, taking out the pilot of the second boat—you did DEVGRU proud out there."

"Screw DEVGRU." His gaze went hard for a moment.

That reaction surprised her, but there were so many

things on her mind that she let it go. "What happens to us now? What happens to Paulito?"

"Tower will be here tomorrow. We'll fly back to Miami and—"

She pressed a finger to his lips. "No, what happens to *us* —to you and me."

He rolled away, sat up. "I care about you, Gabi, but I'm not good with relationships."

Her heart seemed to crack, darkness seeping into her chest. "So, we saved each other's lives, had terrific sex, and that's it? We say goodbye in Miami and move on."

"That's not what I said."

She sat up, rested her cheek against his shoulder, his body tense. "Please tell me what you're thinking."

"Want to hear why I left the Teams?"

She wasn't sure what this had to do with anything. "Tell me."

He turned to face her, both of them sitting on the bed. "Being an assaulter, a member of Blue Squadron, meant everything to me. The Team guys—they were my brothers. I would have gone with them into hell. We spent more time with each other than we did anyone else."

"You must have been very close."

"I thought so." His brow furrowed, his gaze dropping. "Most of the guys were married or divorced with kids. I was the single one. I met Valeria at a bar off base. There are women who hang out there every night, hoping to marry Team guys, but I thought she was different. A year later, we were engaged. I had it made. I was an elite warfighter, I had a beautiful fiancée, and the two of us were expecting a baby."

A baby? He was a father?

What else don't you know about him?

"That sounds like a good life."

"One night, the Team went out, got hammered. We'd just gotten home from a deployment and had lost a guy. Everyone was broken up about it. I sent a text to Valeria, telling her I'd need a ride home. One of my buddies was drunk off his ass. He said, 'She's not home, man. She's with Kruger.'"

"Who's Kruger?"

"He was our squadron commander."

Oh, God.

Gabriela had a terrible feeling she knew where this story was going.

"I took an Uber to Kruger's place. Her car was parked in his driveway. I pounded on the door. He answered, tried to lie his way out of it, standing there in his designer bathrobe. I forced my way inside and found Valeria half-naked in his bedroom."

"I'm so sorry."

"The bastard had been fucking my fiancée while I was deployed. He sent me into combat and fucked my fiancée."

"And the baby?"

"I demanded a paternity test. She resisted at first. The baby wasn't mine, but the two of them were fine with letting me believe it was."

Gabriela remembered his reaction to discovering she was an Agency officer and not a religious sister—the rage, the sense of betrayal.

No wonder he hated being deceived.

"I'm so sorry, Dylan. I can't imagine how that must have felt."

"That wasn't the worst of it." He shook his head, a grim smile on his face. "I found out the next day that the Team guys knew. The married guys—their wives knew. Word got around, but no one bothered to tell me."

Gabriela's heart shattered for him. "You lost everything —your whole life."

"It was all a lie." His gaze met hers again, his eyes shadowed by grief—and anger. "After the paternity test came back, I resigned. I reported Kruger to higher-ups and spent a month drinking. I figured I must have done something to push her away. I must not have been the man she needed."

That's why he thought he wasn't good at relationships.

Gabriela took his hand. "It wasn't you, Dylan. It was Valeria."

"Maybe." He drew a breath, let it go. "Eventually, I sobered up and tried to figure out what to do with my life."

"You found Cobra."

"A friend of mine knew Javier Corbray. He's former DEVGRU also. He and Tower pulled me out of a nosedive, gave me a new purpose."

"Thank you for trusting me with that." Gabriela tried to digest what he'd just shared with her. He'd been with Cobra for five years, so this hurt wasn't new. But it wasn't ancient history either—and it cut deep. "I can't imagine how hard that was, how hurt you must have been. I bet it's been difficult since then to make friends."

Or to trust women.

"Yeah." He took her hand. "I have feelings for you, Gabriela, but I..."

She waited for him to finish, then tried to articulate what he couldn't seem to say. "You're afraid of being hurt again. You find it hard to trust. That makes so much sense, Dylan. But there's one thing you're forgetting."

"What's that?"

She rose onto her knees, kissed him. "I'm nothing like Valeria."

She made love to him then, soft and slow, pouring her heart into every kiss, every caress, trying to show him what she couldn't tell him.

Afterward, they lay together, hearts thrumming, his fingers tracing a line along her spine, the cry of gulls and the pulse of the surf in the distance.

21

"One day you're running from *sicarios*. The next, you're relaxing on the beach in Curaçao, soaking up the sun." Dylan sipped his mai tai, the taste of rum and citrus shimmering over his tongue, the sea and surf calling to him.

"It's surreal, isn't it?" Looking lethally sexy in a low-cut one-piece suit in white, Gabriela ate the cherry from the top of her piña colada. "It feels like a lifetime ago that I was abducted from the mission, but it's only been twelve days."

"A lot can happen in twelve days."

Like falling in love.

They'd slept in, fucked each other's brains out, ordered room service, then bought bathing suits and hit the beach, scoring a couple of reclining chairs not far from the bar. After all that had happened, neither of them felt bad about drinking before noon.

Hell, Dylan needed the alcohol. He was in love with her —and after last night, he was pretty sure she felt the same way. It ought to have been easy, but it wasn't. He should be able to trust her after what they'd been through together.

Then again, he'd trusted his Team guys, and look how that had turned out.

This doesn't have anything to do with trusting Gabriela.

He'd let himself be deceived by the people closest to him, blinded by his love for Valeria and his faith in his SEAL brothers.

It was himself he didn't trust.

He finished his drink, handed it to a server, got to his feet. "I'm going in."

Gabi smiled from behind new sunglasses. "Have fun."

He ran out to the water, dove into the waves, swam against the tide as hard as he could, ignoring the pain in his bruised ribs, until he was maybe a half-mile offshore, alone with the gulls. He stayed there, bobbing on the swells, trying to control the maelstrom of emotions inside him.

You're an idiot if you let what happened with Valeria and Kruger rule your life.

Yes, but how could he be sure this was real? They hadn't even known each other for two weeks. When they got back to the real world and the adrenaline wore off, their feelings might fade, too. Getting caught up in her too soon was risky.

Too late for that, cabrón. *Besides, you take risks for a living.*

But could he take a risk on Gabriela?

Having found no peace in the water, he swam back to the shore, where some blond guy in blue trunks stood talking to Gabriela, drink in his hand.

She waved to Dylan. "There's my boyfriend."

The dude took one look at Dylan, mumbled something, and moved on.

Gabriela removed her sunglasses, her gaze moving over Dylan. "Water running down muscles—I think that's my new favorite art form. Go back, jump in the water, and come out again. Pretty please?"

He appreciated the compliment, but his gaze was still on the jerk in the blue trunks. "Was he hitting on you?"

"I was about to tell him I've killed men, but you scared him off." She sipped the last of her drink. "Every woman on this beach is staring at you, including me."

Dylan grabbed his towel, dried off, and ordered another drink for each of them, trying to find his courage. What was he going to say? He didn't know.

He took hold of Gabriela's hand. "When we get back..."

"Cruz." A shadow fell over them. "We've been busting our asses to get the two of you to safety, and I find you on the beach sipping umbrella drinks."

Tower.

Dylan stood, as did Gabriela. "Glad to see you, too, sir."

Tower held out his hand. "Ms. Marquez, it's a pleasure to meet you at last. I'm glad you're safe."

Gabriela gave him that smile of hers. "Thanks for all you and Cobra did for the hostages and me. I wouldn't be here if it weren't for Dylan."

Was she campaigning for him now? That was sweet.

Dylan couldn't imagine he needed her help. He'd gotten the job done. Yeah, Tower had caught him holding Gabriela's hand just now, but Dylan knew what to say if Tower got his boxers in a twist over that.

"I've got lots of questions. You two finish your drinks and get your gear together. The jet is refueling. We're wheels up for Miami in two hours. There will be a flight waiting there to take you to Langley, Ms. Marquez. Cruz, we'll head on to Denver for a formal debriefing. Meet me in the lobby when you're ready to go."

Gabriela watched Tower walk away. "He seems *very* professional."

"Former Green Beret."

"Aha."

Back in their hotel room, Dylan stripped out of his wet trunks, rinsed the salt off his skin in the shower, and dressed. Gabriela had changed into the black sundress he'd bought her, her other belongings in a shopping bag.

"What were you about to say before Tower walked up?"

It's now or never, buddy.

Once they stepped onto that plane, things would change.

He tried to find the words. "That night after I gave you morphine, you told me you didn't want this to end. You didn't want this to mean goodbye."

"I meant that. I still do. I... care about you, Dylan."

He heard her hesitation. Had she been about to say *love*?

He sat beside her. "What you don't remember is my answer. I said that I didn't want it to end, either."

"You did?"

"Yeah, but you were high as a kite and exhausted. I'm not surprised you don't remember. In fact, I was counting on that."

"Chicken."

It was the truth.

"I'm scared to death, Gabi. I don't know how it could work with the two of us living so far apart, but I can't stand the idea of not seeing you again. I'm not ready for any commitments. I don't know that I ever will be. But I want you in my life. I know that's unfair, but is it enough for you for now?"

She took his hand. "Yes."

And because he couldn't help himself, he drew her close and kissed her.

~

Gabriela had never flown in a private jet before. Comfortable seats. Wet bar. Huge TV screen on one wall. PS4. Restrooms. A conference room. She tried to hide her surprise. "This is ... acceptable."

Dylan wasn't fooled. "It's the only way to fly. Can I get you a drink?"

"What do you have?"

Dylan walked to the bar, opened the refrigerator. "There's beer, water, champagne, ginger ale, Coke, some fancy flavored seltzer."

"Champagne sounds perfect. Shouldn't we be celebrating?"

They were going home—alive and safe.

Then why are you feeling so down?

Dylan.

She didn't know when she'd see him again.

Dylan popped the cork, poured them each a glass, calling to Tower, who was up talking to the pilot. "Hey, Tower, want some champagne?"

"No, thanks."

"Stupid question." Dylan sat beside her. "Cheers."

"Cheers." She sipped, the bright taste tickling her tongue.

Dylan lowered his voice. "I need to get your cell phone number."

"I don't have a cell phone or an email account or any of that."

"Right." He stood, walked into the conference room, and returned with a pad of Cobra stationery. He wrote down his phone number, held onto it for a moment as if hesitating, then handed it to her. "Here's mine."

She took it, his effort warming her. She knew none of this was easy for him. He'd looked more afraid sharing his feelings with her in the hotel room earlier than he had when they'd dragged him off to torture him. "Thanks, Dylan. This means a lot to me."

"Buckle up," Tower called to them. "We're about to take off."

The plane taxied onto the runway, gained speed, and took to the skies.

Gabriela watched out the window as Curaçao became a small island in the middle of a vast turquoise sea, Venezuela in the far distance.

"Hey, are you okay?" Dylan asked.

"I can't believe I'm going home. It's been so long."

Then Tower sat down across from them—a deliberate choice since there was a lot of room and many empty seats. A tall man, he was lean and hard with a tanned face and blond hair, every inch of him the military man.

"You gave me the basics last night over the phone, but I've got a lot of questions that need answers, and some of these questions are for you, Ms. Marquez." He paused as if waiting for their consent, but what choice did they have? "How did you know the Agency asset was going to betray you?"

They went through it all from that point—Gabriela noticing the physical changes in Sander, Sander admitting that he'd been trying to get paid double.

"I had no choice but to eliminate him," Dylan said.

Gabriela knew that weighed on him. They hadn't talked about it, but she knew it just the same. It weighed on her, too, since he'd done it to protect her.

"It was necessary for the success of the mission and your survival." Next, Tower asked about their thwarted attempt to cross the border and getting caught by Ruiz and his men. "They believed you were a nun?"

Dylan grinned. "She can be very convincing."

Tower shot Dylan a quelling look.

Gabriela fought back a smile. "Yes, sir, they did, though I know Ruiz suspected me of knowing something about the drug shipments at the Mission."

Tower nodded. "It was you, Ms. Marquez, who killed Ruiz."

"Yes. I knew that if I didn't act before Sánchez arrived with the reporters, we would fail at our most critical mission objective. I also knew they would keep torturing Dylan until he talked—and then they would kill both of us."

"You're certain he's dead."

"I can confirm that." Dylan described what he'd seen.

All at once, the horror of it hit Gabriela, made the blood rush from her head, leaving her dizzy.

Gunshots. Bodies strewn across the floor. So much blood.

She blinked, found the men watching her. "Sorry. I ... I just..."

"You don't owe anyone an apology." Tower's gaze softened. "What you did—I couldn't have asked for more from one of our operatives."

"Thank you, sir."

Dylan threaded his fingers through hers and picked up the story from there, his touch reassuring. He told Tower how he'd let Imelda go and then blown up the house.

"I didn't have the heart to kill her, and I take full responsibility for that."

"Understood." Tower looked at his notepad. "Then you stole one of Ruiz's vehicles, drove back to the Aveo, and then on to Maracaibo and finally to Coro, where you hired Paulito to bring you to Curaçao."

Dylan answered. "Yes, sir. We stayed in Maracaibo for

one night, so I could take care of Gabriela's graze wound and we could get some sleep."

Tower grinned. "You've made Jones happy—and a little richer. The guys placed bets on how you'd get Ms. Marquez out of Venezuela. Jones said you'd go SEAL on them and head for the water. I think he won five hundred bucks out of it."

Gabriela had to ask. "Who is Jones?"

"Malik Jones. You've met him." Dylan grinned. "He's the big black dude who was my black-market sales assistant."

Gabriela remembered him, of course. "I guess he knows you pretty well."

"I guess he does."

Tower got back to business. "Here are some things you two should know. Ruiz's death has caused serious instability. In the past twenty-four hours, a cartel war has broken out along the border. There have been more than a dozen killings, part of a power struggle."

Gabriela had expected that.

"What I'm about to tell you now is classified." Tower's gaze moved from Gabriela to Dylan and back. "Luis Sánchez has asked the US to enter him into witness protection. He wants to turn state's evidence for the DEA against the cartel and his brother-in-law, who is, as you know, the president of Venezuela."

Gabriela gaped at Tower, trying to grasp what he'd just said. "He... *what*?"

Tower repeated it. "That's what you accomplished by killing Ruiz, Ms. Marquez. The cartel blames Sánchez. He's smart enough to know he won't survive long without help. You did one hell of a job—both of you. Enjoy the champagne. You earned it."

Tower left the two of them alone.

"I can't believe it." Gabriela looked up at Dylan. "Sánchez giving evidence against the Andes Cartel and the president? This could bring the entire regime down."

Dylan smiled, brushed a strand of hair off her cheek. "Maybe you'll be able to go back to Venezuela sooner than you think."

And for the first time in so long, Gabriela felt hope for her parents' homeland.

~

THE FLIGHT to Miami lasted a little more than three hours.

Dylan could see Gabriela's spirits slipping as they prepared to land. "When you get a phone, call me. I've got a lot of time off coming, so I'll be around."

"No missions for a while?"

"Not for a couple of weeks, at least. How about you?"

"I imagine I'll have a few months off. I've got to put my life back together again—find an apartment, get hooked up to utilities and WiFi, buy a car, probably spend some time with my parents here in Miami."

"They'd better give you a medal." He didn't know if the CIA gave medals.

"I don't think they're going to be as pleased with me as Mr. Tower was. If I'd stayed indoors and let them take the journalists, I wouldn't have been abducted. None of this would have happened. You'd have left on the helicopter with the rest of your team."

"Maybe not. We might not have found the hostages. Remember that *you* provided the intel that enabled us to move quickly to rescue them."

Tower looked up from his tablet. "I have a lot of respect for the Agency, but sometimes it can be too focused on narrow objectives. No one on Cobra's team would face a reprimand for trying to protect the lives or freedom of US citizens."

That made her smile. "Thank you."

Dylan lifted her hand to his lips and kissed it. "You've faced scarier assholes. You can take those bastards."

Their flight had no sooner landed than Tower passed on gate information to Gabriela. "An Agency representative is waiting for you there. I'll escort you."

"Thanks." Gabriela shook Tower's hand. "And thank you for all that you and Cobra have done on my behalf."

Dylan waited for Tower to disembark, but the idiot just stood there. "Tower, man, don't you need to use the restroom or something?"

Tower got the hint. "I'll be on the tarmac."

Dylan waited until he was gone, then drew Gabriela into his arms and kissed her, drawing it out, making it last, not wanting to let her go. "I don't know where this will take us, but you are the most amazing woman I've ever met. Don't let those bastards at Langley get you down. I'll be waiting to hear from you."

She smiled, a sheen of tears in her eyes. "Thank you, Dylan, for everything. You risked so much to keep me safe."

"I'd do it all again in a heartbeat." He kissed her again, then walked with her down the stairs to where Tower stood, waiting.

"I'll escort you to your gate," Tower said.

Dylan watched her walk away, so much he'd wanted to say left unsaid.

She glanced back over her shoulder, her gaze meeting his for just a moment before she and Tower entered the special security entrance.

He'd known he'd miss her, but he hadn't expected saying goodbye to hurt.

You've forgotten how much love sucks.

Yeah, there was that.

Dylan walked to the bar, grabbed a beer, tried to get a grip on his emotions.

By the time the plane had refueled, Tower was back.

He sat, buckled in, pinned Dylan with his gaze. "It's against company policy for operatives to become sexually or romantically involved with our clients."

"Who was the first person to break that rule?" Dylan took a drink, waited.

"I'm one of the owners of this company—and your supervisor."

Dylan raised his bottle in a mock toast. "I'm just following your example."

Tower's eyes narrowed. He picked up his tablet and went back to reading.

And that was the end of that conversation.

It was evening by the time they reached Denver, an autumn chill in the air, the mountains white with the first snowfall of the season.

A car was waiting to drive Dylan and Tower to Cobra HQ, where Dylan turned in his weapons and stowed his gear.

Tower met him in the elevator down to the parking garage. "Thank you, Cruz. This clusterfuck could have ruined the company. If that bastard had gotten away with Ms. Marquez, if you'd ended up on the Venezuelan news, if the two of you had been killed, we'd be out of business."

Coming from Tower, this almost constituted a public display of affection.

"Yeah, it was touch and go there for a while."

"You worked the problems one at a time. You trusted your instincts as a warfighter. You powered through it—and so did Ms. Marquez."

"Hell, yeah, she did."

The elevator doors opened.

"See you tomorrow at oh-nine-hundred for an official debriefing." Tower stepped out and walked toward his vehicle.

Dylan drove to his condo in Five Points, grabbed his mail, and let himself in. Rather than going through his usual post-mission routine—laundry, a shopping list, a quick trip to the store—he poured himself a drink and sat in the dark, an ache in his chest.

22

G abriela scanned her ID to enter the elevator and punched the button for the third floor, doing her best to ignore the butterflies in her stomach. Today was her official mission evaluation. She'd worn a conservative gray pantsuit, armor for today's battle. She shouldn't be nervous, but she was.

The past week had been rough. She'd spent most of her time in debriefings that felt more like interrogations, answering the same questions again and again. She knew they were unhappy with aspects of her performance. She couldn't blame them.

She had effectively ended her mission the moment she'd stepped between Pitón and the journalists. Even so, she wasn't sure what she could have done differently. She had reacted on instinct, her mission objectives forgotten the moment she heard the gunshots and screams.

As busy as she was with debriefings, she hadn't had time to look for an apartment or buy a car or shop for more than a few necessities—though she had made sure to get a phone. The Agency had given her temporary housing and a rental car, which helped. But after life as a religious sister—not to mention the abduction and escape from the cartel—it felt strange to be back in the US and out in the world.

Amid the stress of re-entry, Dylan had been her anchor, the sound of his voice enough to smooth all her rough edges. He'd done this so many times—countless deployments followed by a return to the real world. He understood what she was feeling and seemed to know just what to say. They talked about flying together to Puerto Rico or Hawaii or Greece when she was finally given leave.

"It doesn't matter to me where we go as long as there's room service, wine, and you," Gabriela had said.

"That narrows it down a bit," he'd joked.

God, she missed him. She missed everything about him—his voice, his hand holding hers, that smile, those eyes, the warmth of his body beside her at night, the bliss of making love with him.

The elevator door opened with a *ding*, and she made her way to the conference room. Colby, her immediate supervisor, had told her to expect a reprimand but assured her that the evaluation would be fair.

She drew a breath, put on her game face, and stepped through the door, acknowledging each man with a glance and a nod. "Director Walker. Senior Director Rayburn. Assistant Director Colby."

She set her handbag on the floor, took a seat—and waited.

Walker was the first to speak. "How are you feeling? I understand you were shot."

"A graze wound, sir. It's healing well. The doctor removed the stitches and cleared me."

He nodded, his brow furrowing. "You did some extraordinary work during the eighteen months of this assignment. There's no denying that. Your ability to maintain your cover under the most adverse circumstances has been noted. Your talent for improvisation is also impressive."

"Thank you, sir."

"In our assessments during your training, there was nothing to indicate you would perform effectively in a combat situation. We have updated those assessments."

Assistant Director Rayburn took over. "What concerns us was your decision to risk your entire mission in a foolhardy and ultimately failed attempt to prevent the journalists from being abducted."

And now came the reprimand.

"You are a valuable resource," Rayburn said. "Women—people—with your particular set of skills are not easy to find. While your instinct to protect US citizens is laudable, you brought your mission to a premature end and put your life in jeopardy for two people who, quite frankly, ignored State Department travel advisories and had no business being in Venezuela."

"Yes, sir." She couldn't deny it. "I'm sorry, sir. I heard the screams and gunshots and reacted on instinct. At the same time, I was able to protect the hostages and get intel to you that made their rescue—and mine—possible."

"That has been noted," Colby said. "It's in the evaluation. We know—"

Walker cut him off. "It wasn't your job to look after those journalists. Did you forget who you were? You lost yourself in the part you were playing and started thinking like a nun and not an officer. You weren't there on a mission of mercy."

Gabriela fought to keep her temper in check. "I didn't lose myself in any part, sir. That's who I am!"

"That's who you are." Walker repeated her words. "Look

at the consequences of that single act. We had to send your contacts underground in case you were outed as an Agency officer. The Andes Cartel is now caught up in a violent internal struggle, as well as a turf war with neighboring cartels, destabilizing the region. Our only Agency asset inside SEBIN is dead thanks to Cobra, so now we're blind."

He was talking about Sander.

"He betrayed us. He would have turned us over to the cartel."

"Not if you hadn't gotten yourself abducted!" Walker's voice boomed through the small room. "That's my point. If you had remained at the Mission, our asset never would have been involved, and the region wouldn't be caught in a deadly cartel war."

Rayburn cut in. "You have to understand, Ms. Marquez, that your greatest value to the Agency was as an undercover officer in Venezuela. But we can't send you there again. Your face has been on the TV news and in newspapers. We can't assign you to *any* region where the Andes Cartel has operations, which rules out most of Central and South America. If the Andes Cartel survives, they'll be looking for you."

"Yes, sir. I know."

Walker cleared his throat. "Apart from that mistake, your performance was exemplary. From your abduction onward, you exhibited the very best of what an Agency Officer should be. We're giving you a commendation together with a reprimand. Because of you, two US hostages are home safely, a ruthless cartel boss is dead, and Luis Sánchez has come crawling to *our* doorstep, pleading for help."

"He might be the key to regime change," Colby added.

"Let us hope so." Then it might all be worth it.

Rayburn leaned back in his chair. "You've got three

months of hard-earned leave. When you return, we're reassigning you to the Latin American division as an analyst."

Gabriela's heart sank.

There it was—the bottom line. A desk job. She ought to have anticipated this. She'd known she couldn't return to Venezuela. What did she expect them to do?

She hid her disappointment. "I understand. Thank you."

After that, it was just small talk—the weather, what the cafeteria was serving for lunch, the traffic caused by nearby road construction.

Gabriela thanked them and left the building. She made it to the car before the tears came.

DYLAN PARKED AT DIA, jogged inside the terminal, and glanced up at the Arrivals screen. Gabi's plane had already landed.

Damned traffic. I-25 sucked.

He shot her a text message, told her he was here, then made his way to the lobby area to wait, anticipation thrumming in his veins.

It had been only eight days since he'd watched her walk away at the airport in Miami— just eight days—and it felt like a month. Though they'd spoken every night on the phone, it wasn't enough. Any fears he'd had about his feelings for her fading with the danger and adrenaline were gone.

When she'd called yesterday and explained what had happened, he'd told her to get on a plane and come to Denver. Then he'd called Tower and asked for a private meeting. He understood that the Agency had their reasons for reprimanding her, but he didn't give a damn. All they saw were words on a page. They hadn't seen her in action. She didn't have to put up with their bullshit.

The escalator brought a wave of humanity—but not Gabriela.

A grandmother whose grandkids ran to greet her. A soldier home on leave. Business travelers talking on their phones.

He was usually a patient man. As an assaulter and operative, he'd learned to wait. But he didn't feel patient now.

Another full escalator.

His gaze moved over the throng, searching for her.

A hand slid up his spine. "Looking for someone?"

Dylan turned—and there she was, the sight of her sending a rush of pure happiness through him. "God, it's good to see you."

"I've missed you so much." She looked beautiful and very professional in a gray pencil skirt and black blouse, strappy heels on her feet, a little makeup on her face.

He drew her close, smeared her lipstick with a kiss, the feel of her in his arms precious. "I've missed you. I can't wait to get you naked."

"I second that."

Too bad they had a meeting with Tower first.

He drove her from DIA to Cobra HQ and parked in the secured underground garage. He gave her a tour of the building—the front hallway with its walls of polished stainless steel, the glass-walled conference rooms with their built-in blinds, the gym, the breakroom, the shooting range. Then he got her a bottle of water to help with the altitude and grabbed a cup of coffee for himself.

"We've got a full-time armorer who maintains our firearms, but his workshop is locked up for the weekend."

"This is not at all what I was expecting. It's so ... *classy.*"

"I'm glad you think so." Tower stood behind them.

He led them to his office and motioned for them to sit. "Here's what concerns me about bringing you on board here at Cobra. You and Cruz became intimate on this mission. How does that play out down the line if you break up? Will you still be able to work effectively together, or will your personal drama put our operations at risk?"

That was the thing about Tower. He was always direct.

Gabi clearly wasn't intimidated by him. "I understand your concern, sir. You can't have staff bringing their baggage into the office or allowing their emotions to compromise their work. If you offer me a position and I accept, I will act professionally, no matter what's going on in my private life."

Tower's expression gave away nothing. "And, you, Cruz. If Thor Isaksen walks in, and she decides she prefers the tall Norse god look to the Latin lover, how is that going to work for you?"

Those words hit a sore spot inside Dylan, making his body tense, the memory of betrayal hardwired into him. But to his surprise, the twinge of emotion passed, leaving a strange sense of clarity.

"No matter what happens between Gabi and me, she will always be the woman who picked up a rifle and fought her way through a dozen *sicarios* to stop me from being tortured and save my life. I won't forget that. I want her to be happy."

It was the truth.

He loved her.

You should tell her that, cabrón.

Tower nodded, his brow furrowed in thought. "I'll take you both at your word. Ms. Marquez, I'll talk to my partner, Javier Corbray, and get back to you with an offer."

Gabi stared at Tower, clearly surprised. "That's it? No more questions? No resumé? No psych eval?"

Tower chuckled. "We've had our eye on you since we found out you weren't a nun. Your skillset is... *unique*. Compared to you, former elite operators like Cruz are a dime a dozen."

"Hey, I'm right here." Still, Dylan knew it was true.

Tower ignored him. "I've already read through your Agency file, and I am, of course, familiar with your actions in Venezuela. I know you received a reprimand for trying to protect the journalists. I'm not concerned. You're young, and it was your first solo, undercover mission. You ran headlong into danger, not once, but twice—first in an attempt to protect the reporters and then when you saved Cruz. That's who you are."

Dylan could see those words touched Gabi.

"Thank you for understanding, sir."

Tower thanked them for coming in on the weekend, told them he hoped they enjoyed their hard-earned vacation time, and the interview was over.

Gabi was alight with excitement. "Does this mean I'll meet Holly Bradshaw?"

"You'll be her co-worker." But Dylan had more important things on his mind. He nuzzled her cheek, lowered his voice to a whisper. "I need to get the hell out of here—and deep inside you."

"God, yes."

It took all of his willpower to keep his hands off her as they made their way back to his vehicle and drove to his condo. He parked, carried her bag inside, and locked the door behind them, one thing on his mind.

She leaped into his arms, kissed him.

He backed her up against the door, took control of the

kiss, hunger pounding through his veins, his cock already hard.

"Now!" She yanked down his zipper, stroked his erect cock.

He rucked her skirt up to her hips and lifted her off the floor, pinning her against the door with his weight, and moving the crotch of her panties aside.

"*Yes.*" She wrapped her legs around his waist.

He buried himself inside her with a single, slow thrust, the two of them moaning in unison as she took all of him.

No condom this time.

He tried to settle into a smooth rhythm, but she felt too damned good—wet and hot and tight. "Jesus."

His control shredded, he pounded himself into her, hard and fast... needing her... losing himself in the feel of her. He babbled nonsense in two languages. "Gabi, you're so ... *Mi amor*. I need... Fuck! *Eres perfecto.*"

Faster. Harder.

Every thrust made her moan now, her eyes squeezed shut, her lips parted.

He knew she was close, her body going stiff. He fought to relax, to last just that little bit longer, just a little longer for her sake.

"Dylan!" She cried out his name as climax took her, bliss shining on her face.

He let himself go, groaning out his pleasure against her throat as orgasm claimed him and he spilled himself inside her.

GABRIELA LAY against Dylan's chest, the two of them sharing his oversize bathtub, warm water lapping against her breasts, glasses of wine sitting on the ledge. "So, no condom this time?"

"I paid Doc Sullivan—Cobra's staff doctor—a visit last week to get tested. So, yeah, we're good."

"Thank you, Dylan." It warmed Gabriela's heart that he'd taken steps to protect her without being asked.

He kissed the top of her head. "I never want to hurt you."

She was certain he loved her. He was just too afraid to say it.

"Hey, did you see the news last night? The two journalists gave an interview."

She shook her head. "I missed it."

"Dianne Connolly—she went on about you, how brave you were, how you protected them, how you faced down the bastards, and got them to treat her and her photographer better. She told the interviewer that she wasn't sure you were still alive and said she's started going to church because of you. She called you 'fearless.'"

That hit Gabriela right in the heart. "I wish I could call to tell them I'm safe."

"What if you called as Sister María?"

"They're journalists. If they started digging... It's just too risky."

"I guess they'll just have to wonder. What did you think of Tower?"

"That man is laser-focused."

"He's a completely different person with his wife, Jenna."

That made her smile—the former Green Beret being a softie around his wife.

"Will you accept Cobra's offer? It means more money, more time off, lots of travel, more flexibility."

"A part of me is sad about leaving the Agency, but I don't

want to be stuck at a desk all day. It's not what I trained for. I'll accept Cobra's offer—if you're truly okay with us working together. I don't want you to feel like I'm stalking you."

He tickled her ribs. "It was *my* idea."

That was true.

"When we get back from wherever we're going, I'll need to buy a car, find a place to live, and get my stuff out of storage in Virginia."

"You can stay here in the meantime. There's no rush. I've got plenty of room."

He *did* have a lovely condo—two bedrooms, a stylish modern kitchen, three bathrooms, this big tub, a gas fireplace, a balcony facing the mountains.

"Thanks. That's sweet of you."

Was he ever going to say it?

Maybe you should go first.

Great idea—but what if she scared him?

Dylan chuckled again. "Tower, man. I knew he was going to bring up the relationship thing. He mentioned it on the flight from Miami to Denver, reminding me that it's against company policy for operatives to get intimate with clients."

"What did you say?"

"I reminded him that he was the first person at the company to break that rule."

"I can only imagine the look on his face." She laughed. "That question he asked us both—he wasn't testing my response. He was testing *yours*. You know that, right?"

"What?" Clearly, Dylan hadn't picked up on that.

"He wanted to see how you would react. That's why he brought up the Nordic god guy. He was trying to push your buttons to see if he could provoke you."

"That bastard." Dylan gave a little laugh. "I guess that makes sense. He knows why I left the SEALs."

"I could see that his question upset you at first."

"My whole body tensed, and then ... somehow, I just let it all go."

She'd seen that, too.

She sat up, turned to face him, water sloshing over the edge of the tub and onto the stone tile floor. "I want you to know, Dylan, that I would never betray you like that. Despite all evidence to the contrary, I'm a pretty traditional girl. I could never be with one man and hook up with another."

He reached out, ran a wet finger over her cheek. "I meant what I said, Gabi. I want you to be happy, whether you're with me or someone else. The truth is..."

"Tell me." *Please, just say it.*

His jaw tensed, and he took a breath, his gaze meeting hers, gray eyes dark. "The truth is that I'm in love with you, and it scares the hell out of me. I wasn't looking for you, but you found me. I haven't felt this whole or alive in so long. I know that probably sounds crazy."

Gabriela's heart melted, joy washing through her like a sunrise. "It doesn't sound crazy at all—not to me. Some things are just meant to be. I love you, too, Dylan."

"You're my miracle, Gabi."

She set her wine aside, straddled him, caught his face between her palms. "And you're my favorite sin."

Then she kissed him.

EPILOGUE

Six months later

Gabriela waited with Dylan, Lev, and Malik in the living area of a hotel suite at the LA Hilton, the men wearing tailored suits and ties, Gabi in a dark blue skirt suit and heels. This wasn't like any operation she'd been part of for either the Agency or Cobra. Today, they were playing themselves, and Corbray and Tower wanted them to look professional.

"Do you think they'll be disappointed?"

"Disappointed?" Lev arched an eyebrow. "Why would they be disappointed—because you're not a nun?"

Malik glanced up from his phone. "They'll just be happy to see you're alive."

Dylan walked over to where Gabriela stood by the window and drew her into his embrace. "Hey, come here. It's going to be fine."

She leaned into his strength, savored the feel of his arms around her. He'd been her rock these past six months, helping her through the nightmares that had followed their ordeal in Venezuela and doing all he could to make the transition from the Agency to Cobra easier. Everything had worked out.

This would work out, too.

They were taking a big risk, and lives were at stake. But inaction had become just as dangerous. Weeks of preparation had gone into today's meeting—planning, troubleshooting, working through details with the Agency.

"Thanks." Gabriela pressed a kiss to Dylan's lips.

"Hey, get a room—a different room," Malik joked.

Lev stood, walked to the door, looked out the peephole. "They're coming."

A knock.

Then Tower stepped in, Dianne Connolly and Timothy Yang behind him. "Ms. Connolly, Mr. Yang, I'd like to introduce Gabriela—your Sister María."

Dianne's hand flew to her mouth—and she burst into tears.

Tim stared at Gabriela as if she were a ghost.

"I'm so glad to see you both." Gabriela walked over to them, hugged Dianne, and shook Tim's hand. "I've wanted to contact you for a long time, but it just wasn't possible. Please, come and sit. We've got tea and coffee."

Tower introduced the men, using first names only. "Dylan. Malik. Lev. These three made up the reconnaissance team for your rescue—with help from Gabriela."

Dianne and Tim thanked each of them in turn and then sat on the sofa.

Gabriela spoke first. "As Mr. Tower has explained, my life depends on you speaking about this to no one—and not just my life, but the lives of good people in Venezuela, the US, and Peru."

"We understand." Dianne took a tissue out of her handbag, dabbed her eyes. "I thought ... I thought for sure you were dead somewhere. I thought they were going to tell me you'd been killed. I was expecting the worst."

"I'm sorry about that." Tower explained. "We're breaking a bunch of rules to have this face-to-face with you. As I already mentioned, we're doing this for two reasons. The first is that it's important to Gabriela that you not worry. The second is that your continual search for Sister María is a threat to Gabriela's security."

Dianne was nothing if not persistent. She'd come dangerously close to discovering that Gabriela was a US citizen. She'd even tried to interview Mother Beatrice. Both the Agency and Cobra had agreed that something had to be done.

Tim cleared his throat, a telltale sheen in his eyes. "We understand."

Dianne gave a little laugh. "I'm going to hazard a guess here and say you're an agent of some sort and not a nun at all."

Gabriela chose her words carefully. "I was working in Venezuela when we were abducted. I did everything I could to keep you safe and make a bad situation less miserable for you—though it didn't feel like enough."

Okay, she hadn't planned on saying that last part, but it was true.

"If it hadn't been for you..." Tears streamed down Dianne's cheeks again. "Damn it! I told myself I wasn't going to cry."

Gabriela touched a hand to her arm. "It's okay. You've been through an ordeal."

Gabriela had shed plenty of tears of her own since then.

Tim finished what Dianne had tried to say. "If it hadn't

been for you, it would have been so much worse. The way you stood up to them…I wish I'd been that brave."

"I'm glad I was able to help." Gabriela then told them how she'd become aware of the Cobra team across the street and how she'd worked to get information and the key to the doors into their hands.

Tower stepped in. "Gabriela enabled us to rescue you must faster than we otherwise might. She let us know where you were being held, gave us intel about the building and the number of hostiles, and then got us that key."

Dianne gaped at her. "You did all that?"

Dylan chuckled. "Yeah, we were pretty amazed, too."

"I know you said no questions, but… Well, I can't help it." Dianne shrugged. "What happened? Why weren't you on the helicopter?"

Gabriela told her how Pitón had tried to run off with her and how Dylan had stopped him. "But then some paramilitaries arrived and cut us off from the rest of you. We had to hide and then make our way out of the country without Cobra's help. It took us another four days to reach safety."

"I'm so glad you're okay. I've spent every day since then imagining the worst. I've prayed for you every night." Dianne looked embarrassed to admit this. "You're not truly a nun, so you probably think that's silly."

"No, I don't. Thank you. I pray. I've prayed for you, too—both of you."

After that, Gabriela listened to Dianne and Tim talk about the changes in their lives since the abduction, the aftermath of terror. Nightmares. Anxiety. Difficulty focusing. An obsession with news about Venezuela.

"Did you see the headlines?" Dianne asked. "It looks like the president is out. His brother-in-law is giving evidence against him. The all-powerful Andes Cartel that worked with him is in tatters. Things are changing."

Gabriela smiled. "Yes, they are."

Then it was over.

"Thank you so much for today." Dianne hugged Gabriela tight. "Knowing you're safe, whether you're Sister María or not, makes me feel like I'm finally home."

Tim hugged her, too. "We will both be grateful for the rest of our lives for the strength and the kindness you showed us. You redefined the meaning of courage for me."

Then it was Gabriela's turn to fight tears.

DYLAN AND GABRIELA got back to Denver in time to grab some carry-out and a bottle of wine. It was warm enough to eat out on the balcony, the sun setting behind mountains still white with snow, night settling over the city.

Dylan took Gabriela's hand. "You did a good thing today with Dianne and Tim."

"It was good for me, too. I hated the idea of them losing sleep over me. It gave me a kind of closure. I feel like I'm finally able to let Sister María go."

"I liked Sister María. She will always be who you were when I met you."

Gabriela stood, walked over to Dylan, and sat on his lap, her fingers tracing the line of his jaw. "Tell me the truth—did you think lustful thoughts about her?"

"I tried hard not to, but Sister María was *hot*. When I saw that photo of you—of María—in the initial mission briefing, my heart literally skipped a beat."

That made Gabi laugh. "It did? That's so sweet."

"You want to know who turns me on more than Sister María?" He stood, lifting her into his arms. "You do."

He carried her inside to the bedroom, undressed her, watched her expression change as she undressed him, her gaze raking over him.

God, he loved her.

They kissed, sinking to the bed, need for her thrumming through him. They knew each other well now, knew one another's secrets, all the surest ways to please. Dylan made her come with his mouth, making it last until she pleaded with him for release. Then he buried himself inside her, made love to her, long and slow, the two of them falling together into paradise.

Afterward, they lay in bed together, her head on his chest as they talked through the day and the latest news from work. Corbray's special trip to the Vatican to turn over the dossier on Father Alberto, who was now hiding in the jungle. Nick and Holly's announcement that they were expecting their second baby. Word that Paulito and his family were doing well in Florida. The rumors that Cobra's next big job would take Dylan and the rest of the tactical team back to Mazar-e-Sharif.

Then it occurred to him. "Hey, tomorrow's Saturday. We get to sleep in."

"I've got an appointment at nine with that realtor, remember?"

"Why don't you cancel it?"

"I need to find a place to live eventually."

"No, you don't." He'd thought this through over the past few weeks, and it made so much sense. He loved her. He wanted her here. "Stay. Live here with me."

She sat up. "You want to live together?"

He chuckled. "We're already living together, or haven't

you noticed? We've been living together for six months. Let's make it real."

"Are you sure? This is your space, your home."

He sat up, took her hand. "I spent the five years before I met you living here alone. After Valeria, I thought I was better off by myself. It was only after I met you that I realized how empty my life was—all Tinder dates and Netflix."

"That sounds lonely."

It had been, even if he hadn't realized it at the time.

"I didn't think I would ever fall in love again, but you changed that. You showed me what an idiot I'd been to hold onto the past. I don't want you living across town. I like waking up beside you every morning and going to sleep with you at night. Wherever I go in this crazy world, I want to come home to you."

Her face lit up with a smile so beautiful that it sucked the breath from his lungs. "I want that, too. I want that so much."

"Then it's settled, *mi amor*." Dylan kissed her, a soul-deep sense of contentment settling inside him. "Welcome home."

THANK YOU

Thanks for reading *Hard Edge*. I hope you enjoyed this Cobra Elite story. Follow me on Facebook or on Twitter @Pamela_Clare. Join my romantic suspense reader's group on Facebook to be a part of a never-ending conversation with other Cobra fans and get inside information on the series and on life in Colorado's mountains. You can also sign up to my mailing list at my website to keep current with all my releases and to be a part of special newsletter giveaways.

ABOUT THE AUTHOR

USA Today best-selling author Pamela Clare began her writing career as a columnist and investigative reporter and eventually became the first woman editor-in-chief of two different newspapers. Along the way, she and her team won numerous state and national honors, including the National Journalism Award for Public Service. In 2011, Clare was awarded the Keeper of the Flame Lifetime Achievement Award for her body of work. A single mother with two sons, she writes historical romance and contemporary romantic suspense at the foot of the beautiful Rocky Mountains. Visit her website and join her mailing list to never miss a new release!

www.pamelaclare.com